ROMAN GHOSTS

Roman Ghosts

by

Luigi Malerba

⊙⊙⊙⊙

Translated by

Miriam Aloisio & Michael Subialka

Introduction by Rebecca West

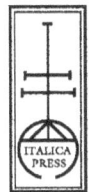

ITALICA PRESS
NEW YORK
2017

Italian Original
Fantasmi romani
© 2006 Arnoldo Mondadori Editore S.p.A., Milano

Translation Copyright © 2017,
Miriam Aloisio and Michael Subialka
Introduction Copyright © 2017, Rebecca West

Italica Press Modern Italian Fiction Series

ITALICA PRESS, INC.
595 Main Street, Suite 605
New York, New York 10044

Library of Congress Cataloging-in-Publication Data
Names: Malerba, Luigi, author. | Aloisio, Miriam, 1980- translator. |
 Subialka, Michael, translator. | West, Rebecca J., 1946- writer of preface. |
Title: Roman ghosts / by Luigi Malerba ; translated by Miriam Aloisio and
 Michael Subialka ; preface by Rebecca West.
Other titles: Fantasmi Romani. English
Description: New York : Italica Press, 2017. | Series: Modern Italian fiction
 | "Italian original Fantasmi romani" -- Verso title page. | Includes
 bibliographical references. | Description based on print version record
 and CIP data provided by publisher; resource not viewed.
Identifiers: LCCN 2016056371 (print) | LCCN 2017011568 (ebook) | ISBN
 9781599103631 (ebook) | ISBN 9781599103617 (hardcover : alk. paper) |
ISBN
 9781599103624 (pbk. : alk. paper)
Subjects: LCSH: Middle class--Social life and customs--Fiction. | Rome
 (Italy)--Social life and customs--21st century--Fiction. | Italy--Fiction.
Classification: LCC PQ4873.A42 (ebook) | LCC PQ4873.A42 F3613 2017
(print) |
 DDC 853/.914--dc23
LC record available at https://lccn.loc.gov/2016056371

Cover Image: Piazza della Rotonda, Rome. Italica Press Archives.

For a Complete List of Titles in
Italian Literature
Visit our Web Site at:
www.ItalicaPress.com

About the Translators

MIRIAM ALOISIO currently teaches Spanish at the University of Colorado Boulder. After finishing her BA in Interpretation and Translation of English and German from the University of Milan, Aloisio earned an MA in Italian Studies from the University of Virginia and a PhD in Romance Languages and Literatures from the University of Chicago with a dissertation on environmental commitment in Luigi Malerba's writing. Her areas of research and teaching include the twentieth- and twenty-first-century novel with a particular focus on postmodern novels, cinematic adaptation, the avant-garde, culture and language. She has collaborated on translations of several literary texts, and she has published and presented on the work of Alessandro Manzoni, Italo Svevo, Elsa Morante, Giorgio Manganelli, Italo Calvino and Luigi Malerba, among others.

MICHAEL SUBIALKA is Assistant Professor of Comparative Literature and Italian at the University of California, Davis. He taught previously at St. Hugh's College, University of Oxford, where he was the Powys Roberts Research Fellow in European Literature, and at Bilkent University in Ankara, Turkey. A scholar of European modernism working at the intersection of literature and philosophy, he has also translated work by Italian authors including Luigi Pirandello, Benedetto Croce, and Bertrando Spaventa. He currently serves as editor of *PSA,* the journal of the Pirandello Society of America.

INTRODUCTION

Malerba is the pen name of Luigi Bonardi (1927–2008), who began to publish fiction in the 1960s after having spent years collaborating on film scripts in Rome where he had moved in 1950 from his home region of Emilia Romagna. A well-respected, even beloved writer in Italy and in many countries around the world where his works have been widely translated, he is surprisingly unknown in North America except to specialists of twentieth-century Italian literature. Only two of his early works have previously been translated into English: *Il serpente* (1966, *The Serpent*) and *Salto mortale* (1968, *What Is This Buzzing, Do You Hear It Too?*), both rendered into wonderfully readable versions by the inimitable William Weaver. But these experimental novels, narratively tricky and demanding, and allied to the Italian neo-avant-garde of the 1960s, were not successes in America, in spite of being very witty and entertaining. Much of Malerba's writing is made up of this mix of challenging and even confounding wiliness and plain old readability. His is an art that questions certainties and complacencies but that also tells a good story. His 2006 *Roman Ghosts,* his last novel, is another such book; ostensibly a recounting, in the alternating sections by both husband and wife, of a bourgeois marriage in trouble, it is, in fact, a much more complex construction, offering a novel within the novel, with shifting boundaries between the real and the imagined, unreliable narrators and two endings. It is also a meditation on urban blight and other contemporary disasters that assail us all. Many of Malerba's trademark elements are present in this novel, and I shall outline some of them towards the end of this brief introduction, although it is not necessary to know what is typically "Malerbian" in order to enjoy this fascinating final work.

Malerba was born in Berceto, a town outside of Parma, in 1927, when Fascism was well established and would remain so until 1943. Malerba was fortunate to be able to avoid serving in the military during World War II due to his young age; instead, after completing high school, he studied law at the University of Parma but soon abandoned that path, first going into advertising and scriptwriting and then becoming a writer of fiction. His move to Rome in 1950 brought him into a milieu of others like himself who lived and moved in artistic, literary and cinematic circles, and the young Malerba thrived. In 1963 the mature but still youngish intellectuals and authors who wished to challenge the status quo came together to form the Gruppo '63, a loosely knit fellowship of writers, musicians and scholars, which counted Umberto Eco among its members. Malerba was drawn to their debates and to their goal of renewing artistic modes of expression. The two early novels mentioned above emerged from that heady environment of experimentalism and are, in fact, among the few texts of the so-called Italian "neo-avant-garde" that have stood the test of time, never having gone out of print in the fifty years since their initial publication. Malerba subsequently co-founded the Cooperativa Scrittori (Writers' Cooperative) in 1973, an alternative to mainstream publishing houses. He was also involved in literary journals, such as *Il cavallo di Troia* and *Alfabeta,* some of the most engaging venues for creative and critical work of those years.

A prolific writer, Malerba consistently contributed to newspapers such as *La Repubblica* over the course of his career, and in addition to novels he wrote children's books, short stories, travel pieces and criticism. His work enjoyed the attention of the best critics in Italy and won many prizes (the Mondello in 1987, the Grinzane Cavour Prize in 1989, the Flaiano Prize in 1990, the Viareggio in 1992, the Premio Brancati in 1979, the Premio Feronia in 1992), including the first Médici Prix Étranger given by France to a non-French writer for *Salto mortale* in 1970.

He enjoyed a long marriage (1962 to his death) with Anna Lapenna, with whom he had two children, Pietro and Giovanna, and in addition to inhabiting a wonderful apartment near the Piazza Navona, the family spent much time at their villa and farm, Settecamini, outside of Orvieto where Malerba could go on connecting with the farming roots of his rural Emilian ancestors.

A lover of travel and a generous interlocutor, Malerba visited many countries, often invited by universities and cultural centers to give talks and readings about and from his works. The wide translation of his books meant that students and scholars of Italian literature and general readers in France, Germany, Spain, but also Japan and other non-European countries could read him and come to love his fictional creations. In spite of their often mind-bending challenges to the complacent reader, his books are also user-friendly, filled with humor, wit, and relatable concerns and characters, and so he developed a following that was global in reach. In 2016, his standing as a modern classic was recognized by the publication of a selection of his works in the distinguished Mondadori Meridiani series, devoted to the giants of Italian literature.

Malerba's first fictional work, *La scoperta dell'alfabeto* (The Discovery of the Alphabet) appeared in 1963, the same year in which the neo-avant-garde group known as the Gruppo 63 had its first meeting of writers and critics in Palermo. The volume is a collection of short stories whose protagonists are peasants from the plains around Parma (Malerba's region of origin) and whose temporal setting is the Second World War. It might seem that Malerba's choice of setting and characters in these stories would align them with certain Neorealist techniques and themes, but his tales move far from the tenets of any recognizable realism, into the estranging elements inherent in life and so wittily used by Malerba throughout his career. In the first story, which gives the volume its title, Ambanelli, an old peasant, wants to learn to read and write, but he soon puts into question the logic of the alphabet. Using the technique of estrangement à la Brecht, Malerba challenges a basic given of language, which is itself allied with the structures of power that control and shape society. With the astuteness of a practical man who doubts anything that seems to be without purpose or reason, Ambanelli, whose name suggests "ambivalence" or "ambiguity," asks the boss's son, who is giving him reading lessons, why the letters are in the order they are. The boy can only respond that it is for convenience's sake, but Ambanelli is not satisfied, and maintains his view of the alphabet as "illogical." Nonetheless, he learns enough to be able to write his name and to recognize one hundred or so words, which he greets as old friends when he sees them in print. This story is, in retrospect, emblematic of what will become one of the most Malerbian of qualities, the putting into question of the very instrument of his art: language itself. In fact, Malerba is an author of works that contain many more questions than answers, and he always seeks to create a certain sense of unease in his readers, who are forced to rethink "common sense" and many givens of everyday life, even the alphabet.

As critic Maria Corti noted in her study *Il viaggio testuale* (1978, The Textual Voyage), Malerba's most typical protagonists do not appear in his first book. It is only in his second and in some subsequent works that a type of protagonist is born who will become recurrent: the neurotic, even psychotic, visionary, who has a very peculiar view of reality and a very particular mode of self-expression. Malerba first creates such a protagonist in his 1966 debut novel, *Il serpente*. He tells a very confounding story, which is a sort of mystery tale made up of bizarre occurrences as recounted from the first-person, paranoid perspective of the main character. This man ostensibly has a love affair with a woman named Miriam, for example, but she may well be a figment of his imagination. He asserts specific facts about his wife, only to proclaim later that he never had a wife. The novel ends up negating all of its own assertions, and we are left with a book that has consumed itself like a serpent devouring its own tail, just as the protagonist maintains that he has consumed Miriam in a cannibalistic act motivated by his overpowering desire to possess her completely.

Malerba's second novel, *Salto mortale,* has as protagonist one "Giuseppe called Giuseppe," who believes that he has discovered a murder, which he himself may or may not have committed. Again using the *giallo* or mystery-story mode, Malerba constructs a labyrinthine world of multiple "Giuseppes" and a woman whose name constantly transforms from one Rose-based appellation to another.

In these and other early novels and stories, Malerba uses a number of estranging techniques that keep realism at bay: obsessive repetition of words and phrases, excessive use of the interrogative form, extensive digressions, constant shifts from indirect to direct discourse. An extreme example of estrangement is a talking phallus as protagonist in the novel, *Il protagonista* (1973, The Protagonist). Humor is also employed, but it is of the sort that renders readers uneasy, just like the author himself, who stated that he often wrote in a state of great uneasiness. Malerba can be described as a "psychosomatic" writer in the sense that his cerebral word play originates and is often allied to the physicality of allergies, sex, sneezing and explosive laughter. Both the body and the mind are always in play.

During the 1970s, Malerba was very prolific, writing a number of collections of short stories, novels and books for children. His diverse interests are evident in the range of themes in these works: ancient China in *Le rose imperiali* (1974, The Imperial Roses); the Middle Ages in *Il pataffio* (1978, Mish Mash) and *Storie dell'anno Mille* (1973; Stories of the Year One Thousand), which he wrote with Tonino Guerra; bourgeois life in contemporary Rome in *Dopo il pescecane* (1979, After the Shark); children's classics in *Pinocchio con gli stivali* (1977, Pinocchio in Boots).

From the early novels and short stories written during the 1960s when Malerba, like many other Italian authors, was deeply involved in neo-avant-garde and neo-experimental techniques, and from the eclectic works of the 1970s, the writer moved in the 1980s toward an explicit consolidation of his abiding interest in dreams, as well as in politics and historical writing. *Diario di un sognatore* (1981, Diary of a Dreamer) and *Il pianeta azzurro* (1986, The Blue Planet) are, respectively, a record of the author's dreams as dreamed over a year and a prescient novel about contemporary political corruption à la Tangentopoli, the scandals that hit Italy shortly after the book appeared.

It was in 1980 that the wonderfully witty, little collection of aphoristic stories entitled *Le galline pensierose* (The Pensive Hens) appeared, a book that Italo Calvino called "zen-like" in its transcendence of logical strictures into a stratosphere of oddly convincing "hen logic." For example, in one piece, a hen wishes to ride a tricycle but believes she cannot because she does not have three legs!

In the 1990s, Malerba displayed a strong interest in writing historically-based fiction in which, however, his penchant for contestation, the interrogation of givens and the exploration of the strangeness of the real continued. Novels such as *Il fuoco greco* (1990, Greek Fire) and *Itaca per sempre* (1997, Ithaca Forever) reveal Malerba's historical bent. Both books make extensive use of historical sources, albeit heavily fictionalized. In 1996, a collection of essays concerning the role of the intellectual and of the writer in modern society appeared under the title *Che vergogna scrivere* (How Shameful It Is to Write). The short pieces included in that volume are among some of the most acute observations on the decline of the intelligentsia's leadership across time, as art and the life of the mind have been pushed more and more to the margins of Western society.

Always an enthusiastic voyager, Malerba published volumes in which his curiosity about, and affection for, foreign travel are displayed in lively essays and personal anecdotes. *Il viaggiatore sedentario* (1993, The Sedentary Traveler) and *Città e dintorni* (2001, Cities and Surroundings) are examples of this side of Malerba's ever active and inquisitive intelligence. His later work includes *Il circolo di Granada* (2002, The Circle of Granada), a novel set in nineteenth-century Spain; *La composizione del sogno* (2002, The Composition of the Dream), which gathers together his writings on dreams, one of his topics of abiding interest; and *Ti saluto filosofia* (2004, I Greet You, Philosophy), a collection of essayistic stories in which Malerba's disconcerting comic sensibility is joined to his deeply philosophical bent. Posthumously published works include *Parole al vento* (2008, Words in the Wind), *Diario delle delusioni* (2009, Diary of Disappointments) and a reissue in 2011 of his early repertory of Emilian dialect terms entitled *Le parole abbandonate* (Abandoned Words).

When I went to meet and interview Malerba for the first time in 1985, he and Anna, his wife, were at their farm and told me that they would meet me at the train station in Orvieto. I had come to imagine what the writer must be like, as the creator of highly unreliable — even psychopathic — narrators and the spinner of intricate tales, which often refused to give us readers reassuring dénouements. I saw him in my mind's eye as a bit wild-eyed and ruffled, possessed by the manias of his characters, slippery and odd. I could hardly believe my eyes when I realized that the staid, lawyerly-looking man standing quietly on the platform next to his elegant wife was Malerba. I was further surprised as we began to talk, for he was not at all verbose or flamboyant. Rather, he spoke in a soft pleasant tone and projected a sort of shyness that put my own nerves to rest. Like Nabokov, who was identified with *Lolita*'s Humbert Humbert much to his dismayed amusement, Malerba commented on the phenomenon of readers' mistaking his (especially first-person) characters for the author himself. In *Che vergogna scrivere,* he wrote that "I've often written tales in the first person, an artifice that has fostered more than one misunderstanding and some deplorable identifications [of the author with the character]." Yet the wily writer also often insisted that readers needed to be diffident of authors (or at least of him) because in narrations (at least in *his* narrations), there is always some hidden trick, including techniques of blurring the separation of narrator from character. Examples of Malerbian tricks include his assertion in the novel *Le pietre volanti* (The Flying Stones) that Dürer is among the painters who never painted any flowers, and his revelation after the publication of the novel *Salto mortale* that it was written in verse, although published as if only in prose.

This brings us back to *Roman Ghosts*, a novel of apparent simplicity but in fact of wily complexity. Giano and Clarissa have consciously "maintained" their marriage (as one maintains a car) for twenty years through the tacit use of mutually agreed-upon hypocrisy, lying and infidelities. This *modus vivendi* has resulted in an "imperfect balance," but one that has permitted them to go on being together. Giano is a rather obsessive professor of architecture who focuses on urban planning. His great project is called "Urban Deconstruction" and would involve demolishing ten percent of the neighborhoods built in Rome since 1940 in order to allow for better air circulation and more green space. When Giano decides to write a novel based on his and Clarissa's lives, he hides it in a folder marked "D. U." (Decostruzione Urbanistica) so that his wife will think it contains notes for his deconstruction project and will not pry into it. Yet he also leaves the folder sitting out in full view so that Clarissa will be at least somewhat tempted to look into it, which indeed she does. As she reads the novel, she begins to believe that Giano knows all about her affair with the architect Zandel, and in fact seems to be predicting accurately the course of that affair.

As we read *Roman Ghosts*, which is made up of short chapters recounted in ping-pong fashion alternately by Giano and Clarissa, we begin to see that Giano's novel is a more or less exact re-creation of the events taking place in the novel by Malerba, and we thus begin to wonder where one novel begins and another ends. The two works intermingle, spreading echoes and repetitions, becoming more and more a veritable *mise en abyme* or meta-novel that, like earlier works of Malerba, devours itself as it goes along. The ending does not clarify what is "true" (that is, written by Malerba in a straightforward narrative about a marriage) or "imagined" (that is, written by Giano in his narrative within the narrative, which is a fantasy of revenge on his unfaithful wife), because two endings that contradict one another are offered. Like the two-headed eagle of the joke that opens the novel and the two-faced Giano or Janus, the double-faced god who looks both backwards and forwards, Malerba's novel is rife with doubleness and duplicity in its very structure, just as its characters are duplicitous and double-dealing.

There are typical Malerbian elements in this novel, including the figure of the architect, who in some sense stands in for the authorial presence who controls all in his constructed universe; references to Malerba's earlier works; constant questioning; meditations on what narratives are and how they work; shifty, sly humor; witticisms; abundant use of the urban geography of the author's beloved/hated Rome; a touch of the mystery or crime novel; concerns of a socio-political nature like the spread of AIDS or environmental pollution. But there is nothing repetitive or tired about this final novel. It beckons us in with its urbane readability, only to capture us in its web of deceit, built on the most masterly manipulation of narrative structure and, in a word, of *words*, Malerba the "architect's" chosen instrument for the creation of an inimitable hall of mirrors all his own. To enter it in this fine translation is to discover just how engaging an author Luigi Malerba is, and just how much reading pleasure awaits future ventures into his narrative universe.

Rebecca West, University of Chicago

Works of Luigi Malerba

Novels and Essays

Il serpente (Bompiani, 1966)

Salto mortale (Bompiani, 1968), winner of the Prix Médicis

Il protagonista (Bompiani, 1973)

Le parole abbandonate (Bompiani, 1977)

Il pataffio (Bompiani, 1978)

Diario di un sognatore (Einaudi, 1981)

Il pianeta azzurro (Garzanti, 1986), winner of the Premio Mondello

Il fuoco greco (Mondadori, 1990)

Le pietre volanti (Rizzoli, 1992), winner of the Viareggio Prize and the Premio Feronia

Le maschere (Mondadori, 1994)

Che vergogna scrivere (Mondadori, 1996)

Avventure (Il Mulino, 1997)

Interviste impossibili (Piero Manni, 1997)

Itaca per sempre (Mondadori, 1997)

La superficie di Eliane (Mondadori, 1999)

Proverbi italiani (Istituto poligrafico dello Stato, 1999)

Città e dintorni (Mondadori, 2001)

La composizione del sogno (Einaudi, 2002)

Il circolo di Granada (Mondadori, 2002)

Le lettere di Ottavia (Archinto, 2004)

Ti saluto filosofia (Mondadori, 2004)

Fantasmi romani (Mondadori, 2006)

Il sogno di Epicuro (Manni, 2008)

Parole al vento (Manni, 2008)

Diario delle delusioni (Mondadori, 2009)

Raccomandata Espresso (Edizioni dell'Elefante, 2009)

Romanzi e racconti, saggio introduttivo di Walter Pedullà, Collana I Meridiani, Milano, Mondadori, 2016

SHORT STORIES

La scoperta dell'alfabeto (Bompiani, 1963)

Le rose imperiali (Bompiani, 1974)

Dopo il pescecane (Bompiani, 1979)

Testa d'argento (Mondadori, 1988), winner of Grinzane Cavour Prize

TRAVEL

Cina Cina (Piero Manni, 1985)

Il viaggiatore sedentario (Rizzoli, 1993)

CHILDREN'S BOOKS

Mozziconi (Einaudi, 1975)

Pinocchio con gli stivali (Cooperativa Scrittori, 1977, poi Monte Università Parma, 2004)

Storiette (1978)

Le galline pensierose (1980)

Storiette tascabili (1984)

WITH TONINO GUERRA

Millemosche mercenario (Bompiani, 1969)

Millemosche senza cavallo (Bompiani, 1969)

Millemosche fuco e fiamme (Bompiani, 1969)

Millemosche alla ventura (Bompiani, 1969)

Storie dell'anno Mille (Bompiani, 1970)

Millemosche innamorato (Bompiani, 1971)

Millemosche e il leone (Bompiani, 1973)

Millemosche e la fine del mondo (Bompiani, 1973)

PLAYS

WITH FABIO CARPI
I cani di Gerusalemme (1988)

FILM

1952 *Il cappotto*, directed by Alberto Lattuada

1967 *La ragazza e il generale*, directed by Pasquale Festa Campanile

1967 *Lo scatenato*, directed by Franco Indovina

1968 *Sissignore*, directed by Ugo Tognazzi

1969 *Toh, è morta la nonna!*, directed by Mario Monicelli

1970 *L'invasione* (*Invasion*), directed by Yves Allégret

1970 *Appuntamento col disonore*, directed by Adriano Bolzoni

1972 *Corpo d'amore*, directed by Fabio Carpi

1972 *Il vero e il falso*, directed by Eriprando Visconti

1978 *Come perdere una moglie e trovare un'amante*, directed by Pasquale Festa Campanile

1994 *La prossima volta il fuoco*, directed by Fabio Carpi

ROMAN GHOSTS

◉◉◉◉

Do not worry, gentlemen,
the bourgeoisie is immortal.
Joseph Roth

CLARISSA

There is an eagle's nest on a tall rocky wall. A double-headed eagle flies up to it, astonishing the little community. Finally, someone from the group approaches it and asks:

"Genetic engineering?"

"No, Habsburg."

A friend told us this little story just like that, unembellished. He was a journalist from the *Frankfurter Allgemeine* who had come to Italy to attend a biotechnology conference in Spoleto on behalf of his newspaper. We hosted him for two days in our country house in Casole, near Todi. Before he returned to Germany, Johannes Westerhoff said as a joke that he was giving us the exclusive rights to this little story.

Since then Giano never misses a chance to bring up the double-headed eagle story with his friends. The story is successful for two reasons: it makes reference to a fashionable scientific subject, and it plays on the historical snobbery of the audience. Every time he tells it, Giano introduces new variations, not so much in the narrative plot, which is very simple and rigid, but in the background elements. For instance, one time, it's raining: whoever is listening naturally expects an outcome relating to the rain, and instead the punch line comes like the crack of a whip.

Later Giano realized that at a certain elevation snow is more natural than rain. So he turns it into snow. Other times he says that the eagle is tired — we don't know yet that it's double-headed, since in the joke we see it flying in a long shot — because it comes from a faraway country (Austria?). The secret, Giano says, lies in creating a different expectation than what actually ends the little story: "*peripeteia*," according to Aristotle, which means developing a scene in the opposite direction of what was expected. From presumed genetic engineering to Aristotle, all to end up with a joke (Giano, however, forbade me to call it a joke).

Four days after he left, we learned that our German friend died in a car accident on the road between Frankfurt and Duisburg. He lived in Frankfurt, and he was going to give an informational presentation about the Spoleto conference at Duisburg's rigorous university, which is named after Gerhard Mercator. We were absolutely dismayed by such a stupid death, as all deaths in car accidents are. Poor Johannes, he died after walking the earth for only forty-seven years, in the moment of his peak activity and professional success. We sent a telegram and also mailed a card to his wife, who we knew was in total despair.

How long does the sorrow for a friend's death last? The witty German journalist was more an acquaintance than a real friend, but his death had caught us off guard, and we didn't have anything to say because silence seemed the best expression of our sorrow. His death had elevated him to the rank of friend.

Giano continued to tell the double-headed eagle story but with a subconscious feeling of embarrassment since the story's source went dead. I listened to Giano go on performing the story of the double-headed eagle, and I felt that the air had changed. In my ears I heard the loud death of poor Johannes, a crash of metal sheets on nocturnal asphalt and the desperate voice of a dying man. I would have liked to tell Giano to forget about the double-headed eagle, but I was afraid of hurting his feelings, as if I were scolding him for his lack of sensitivity. Giano recounted the story on three or four more occasions, and each time, while I was listening to his words, in my ears I heard the far away crash of metal sheets on the road between Duisburg and Frankfurt. But I pretended I was having a good time as usual so as not to hurt his feelings.

Giano is very focused when it comes to topics related to urban planning, the subject he teaches in the Department of Architecture of Valle Giulia. But he is extremely naïve in his human and social relationships. Telling these little stories — or paradoxes as he insists on calling them — gives Giano the chance to participate during convivial get-togethers at his friends' or at our house. Above all, it is how he avoids those Four Shitheads who appear on TV and in the newspapers, who always cause him serious allergic reactions, whooping cough and shortness of breath of the asthmatic variety. That's why, following our doctor's advice, I always keep a bottle of Benadryl at home or in my purse when we travel. Cortisone and adrenalin are the only remedies in case of anaphylactic shock. It happened once to Giano one evening, when the First of the Four appeared on TV, with his chest inflated like a turkey, "convinced he was making History and not a pile of Shit," as Giano said in a daring quip just before passing out.

I have to add that in all his versions, whether with rain or with snow, Giano knew how to be elegant in telling that little story I recounted in just a few lines at the beginning. He always managed to create a horizon of expectation by describing the little community of noble birds of prey as if he had seen it in person, as if he shared in the resident eagles' surprise when the wandering eagle

LUIGI MALERBA

with two heads arrived. The most recent time, during lunch with his architect friends, he even informed them of the double-headed eagle's wingspan: just over seven feet. According to ornithology manuals this is the measurement of the Royal Eagle that would be entitled to the appellation "Imperial Eagle" in this particular circumstance (Habsburg).

Giano has already forgotten about poor Johannes Westerhoff and the horrible accident in which he lost his life. Not me. I am still oppressed by the obsessive crash of metal sheets. And I am upset by the memory of my useless reproaches for the cigarettes he smoked continuously: two packets a day of those lethal Marlboros. I was worried about his lungs, poor dear Johannes.

Giano is happily distracted. I mean, his distraction never caused him damage, nor did it damage those around him. Two nights ago, at the house of his fanatical, Taliban architect friends — whom I hate just as much as they hate all that is old — he was about to tell the double-headed eagle story for a second time. I sent him a silent warning: a frowning forehead and a low gaze. Giano understood immediately, and he changed the subject. And now, please, don't think that Giano is an idiot. He's just incorrigibly naïve. That much is true.

I've called him Giano instead of Gianantonio ever since we got married about twenty years ago, twenty-two to be precise. Now everybody calls him Giano, even at the university. Malicious people say that I subconsciously gave my husband the name of the double-faced Roman god, Janus, because of an assumed duplicity of personality and behavior. For goodness sake! The nickname is completely innocent and accidental, created by the contraction of the name Gianantonio, which was tattooed on his forehead since birth. So much conjecture about a name! Call him Giano, I said to myself without thinking about it too much.

Here's how the double-headed eagle story inserted itself like an iron nail into the imperfect balance that sustains our marriage. I said imperfect on purpose because both Giano and I avoid investigating the secrets and the nails that we both carefully guard. Once unburied, they could cause a catastrophe. Lies are our salvation. They maintain our marriage. Sometimes I even lie to myself. It is like a Zen exercise that cheers me up from the rough and oppressive presence of reality.

For instance, I tried really hard to erase Giano's relationship with Patricia from my memory. Patricia is the voracious widow of his colleague, and she kept a certain number of her husband's projects and documents. She wanted to know whether it was possible to publish them somewhere, for example in the journal *Diagonale,* edited by the Architecture Department, and in any case whether Giano could help her catalogue them. Giano complained to me about the hassle, but he couldn't say no to the poor widow. And in the meantime poor Patricia was sleeping with him, as I found out from a friend who collected the dirty woman's secrets. Two months of afternoon sex from three to five. For another two months, instead of being at the library of Palazzo Venezia, he was again at Patricia's place in Piazza dei Mercanti in Trastevere, on the third floor of an old, rickety building. Daily cheating, a real sexual cornucopia. Who knows? It might be all made up. Just malicious gossip. Don't investigate, I told myself. Leave things as they are. Rather bad.

During the days when Giano is busy with his classes at Valle Giulia, I certainly don't stay at home like a mole. First I have the urge to go out in the street — I feel it in my shoes. They drag me toward the door. I go out and walk around the city at random. An exhibition, a stroll along the shop windows in Via Frattina, a supermarket, sometimes a movie downtown, at Capranica or Quirinetta, a gelato in Piazza Navona or at the Pantheon. I also like to wander around the city. I walk at a fast, light pace, looking for shaded areas in the summer, avoiding the gaps in the cobblestones to save my heels. I know the condition of all the cobblestones on the streets of the entire historical center by heart. To be avoided absolutely: Via Giustiniani, Piazza dei Caprettari, Via Tor Millina and Via Arco della Pace. I left a heel in Trastevere between two cobblestones on Via di San Francesco a Ripa. I will have to decide finally to wear the yellow, flat Superga sneakers that Zandel the architect gave me — there were some qualms on account of my average height (only five foot, three-and-a-half inches tall), which makes the two-and-a-half inches of my usual heels advantageous.

I find Via di San Francesco a Ripa to be the most beautiful street in Trastevere with its wonderful little square and the church providing a backdrop at the end of the road. I went back there to find a store for organic products. I wanted to buy an organic soy sauce to replace our Kikkoman sauce, which I'm sure must be produced with GMO soy. I couldn't find the organic store, but I did find my heel still there, trapped between two cobblestones more than a month later. I recall how that day, crippled as I was, I interrupted my wanderings through that part of Trastevere to search for a taxi. That day I realized I would like to live in that area. This street has so much air and so much light. They are already planning to repave it, so I will no longer have to fear for my heels. I am tired of my house on Via del Governo Vecchio now that a jungle of bars has sprung up around the noble Café della Pace. They are popular with the worst, loud night crowd. But that heel — that heel trapped between the cobblestones in Via di San Francesco a Ripa — could be the sign that fate is calling me to that neighborhood. I will start talking with Giano about the idea of moving there. A heel that was trapped right there must mean something, don't you think?

There's too much history cemented in our house on Via del Governo Vecchio, too much dust. You get to a point where you say "enough," and you want to move. Relocations renew life. It is a healthy mix of neurons and hormones. I am always happy to go out. Sometimes I go in a rush, without a reason. When I am in a good mood I feel like I am walking downhill. My pace is light, as if I had wings on my shoes like the god Mercury. When my pace is tired, and all the streets are uphill, I wonder whether I'm in a bad mood, and I say to myself that yes, I am in the worst mood possible. I have plenty of reasons. Believe me, when I say that I'm in a bad mood, I am not exaggerating.

I often run into my girlfriends on the streets downtown, because it's been over twenty years – too many – that Giano and I have lived on the top floor of an old building in Via del Governo Vecchio. That's here in the Parione neighborhood, which has its social center in Piazza Navona and its luxury market center in the Campo dei Fiori. One encounter happened *extra moenia*, outside the city center. At the Tamara de Lempicka exhibition at the French Academy near Trinità dei Monti, I ran into Valeria. We both found ourselves incognito in front of the same painting, both mesmerized, admiring a man wearing a coat and a hat, his elbow leaning on a honey-colored luxury car with a long hood and big lights. It might have been an Isotta Fraschini. It wasn't just the car that had the look of the twenties, but also the man's camel hair coat, his soft Borsalino hat and particularly his face with its thick grey moustache. This is a man I like, I was thinking, or better yet, that I would have liked if I had lived in those years.

With my eyes wide open, looking at the painting, I daydreamed of a romantic ride together through the Tuscan countryside in the sun. I imagined fast Italian kilometers along vineyards and cypress-lined roads with the crisp air caressing my face and finally arriving at a villa among the trees on a hill that welcomes us with a wide-open door. We enter, running. We rush up the stairs, overwhelmed by desire, arriving in the big bedroom. We fling ourselves onto the bed and make love screaming like two wild mammals.

At the French Academy, next to me, side by side, there was a young woman who was also captivated by the same painting. She was still and quiet, perhaps immersed in the same lustful thoughts — I cheated on Giano in front of that painting, with that marvelous specimen of a man from the twenties, with his grey moustache and camel hair coat. Suddenly I turn towards her, and she towards me. It's Valeria. We've known each other for ages, but we never spent time together — only accidental encounters, like this one. Divorced after one year of marriage, Valeria has lived a libertine life ever since. Even today, at over forty, she happily dedicates herself to healthy encounters of erotic recycling, recovering her old relationships. They say that she never passes up the chance with any man who comes her way. It doesn't matter whether they are single or married. When she can, she prefers younger men. According to common opinion, she is a lovable tramp.

Anyway we exchanged some comments about the exhibition. We were both more enthusiastic about those men from the twenties, sleekly presented by Lempicka with love, than about the paintings that looked like posters. Once we exhausted the subject, we had no more to say, and suddenly, I don't know from what obscure impulse, I asked Valeria whether she knew the story of the double-headed eagle, which is short and quick and perfect for social occasions.

"I do," she answered. "Very funny."

It's weird that she knows it, I said to myself, and I asked her who had told her.

Valeria started panicking for a moment, then she got a grip.

"A German friend, a few days ago."

"So," I asked her, "did you happen to know Johannes Westerhoff?"

"No, who is he?"

"The one who told it to us. A journalist from the *Frankfurter Allgemeine*."

"No, I don't know him. I heard it from a Deutsche Bank agent I met in Todi at some friends' house."

Valeria's embarrassment and her rush to interrupt the conversation and leave made it clear she was lying. Why was she lying? It's obvious: because my husband had told her the story, and of course he never even dreamed of mentioning to me that he had seen Valeria. What am I supposed to make of it, if he hid his encounter with Valeria? The worst. Careful though, I can't let myself be overwhelmed by negative feelings of jealousy. It is possible that Giano told her over the phone. Or perhaps it was the Deutsche Bank agent. Why not?

Calm down, I say to myself, calm down Clarissa.

Giano

She's an idiot, a total idiot. Who knows why Valeria told Clarissa that she knew the double-headed eagle story. She fell right into a common trap, the idiot. And why on earth did she say that an agent from Deutsche Bank had told her? As I explained to her, this second stupid mistake is worse than the first one because it needlessly highlights the German provenance of the story and above all because the agent from the German bank really exists, and he, too, has a house near Todi. So Clarissa could easily get a hold of him. Then I would really be in trouble, but luckily I can count on my wife's laziness and perhaps on her desire not to know what she already knows, whether I see Valeria or not.

Clarissa didn't tell me that she met Valeria at the French Academy. But ever since she found out that I told Valeria the double-headed eagle story, Clarissa continues to pressure me with false jealousy, which nonetheless could also be a sign of real affection. In the end these are hypocritical performances. It's acting out our marital theater, a performance of love.

When I teach my classes at the university I keep my cell phone off, so she sends me short texts. "Call me after class." If I don't call her after class, when I get home she won't leave me alone. "Why didn't you call me?" "Where have you been?" "Whom did you see?" "Do you have any cute students in your sights?" Clarissa puts on a wily face that says she has understood everything but already forgiven me. The truth is simpler: Clarissa is very smart, and she has understood that there is nothing to understand when it comes to my students. I am also in love with her for these generous fictions. How boring it would be without Clarissa.

"In what sights and which students? Oh please." I know she's just putting on a show to avoid the real discussions that neither of us wants to deal with. Neither of us wants to open the door to the Four Horsemen. I answer carelessly, which is the easiest way to nullify her false jealousy, which might hide a real jealousy. Who knows? We have always lived in deceit, and we like it this way. It is convenient for both of us. And then that damned double-headed eagle story forced Clarissa to become suspicious of my secret meetings with Valeria. Wait a second! I actually believe Clarissa already knew but pretended not to know. Now she can't pretend as before, which means she's changed the register of her pretense. Clarissa knows perfectly well that Valeria never passes up an opportunity and that if we met up once, what comes next is as sure as two and two is four.

Why didn't Clarissa tell me that she met Valeria at the Lempicka exhibition? She told me about the exhibition enthusiastically, about the charming men and women of the twenties, cars included. Surely Lempicka liked men very much. You can tell from her paintings, full of handsome men who are always elegant. Perhaps Clarissa is better off believing that the man from Deutsche Bank, and not me, really did tell Valeria the double-headed eagle story. That is why she will never investigate the truth with the man from the German bank, because she knows that the truth is inconvenient. It would be the beginning of the break — let's say it — the beginning of a catastrophe, which neither of us wants. We are both in love with each other and, as Clarissa says, maintaining our marriage is a categorical imperative.

I absolutely don't believe that Clarissa is cheating on me. I repeat it to myself every day. But I also know that for every assertion its contrary is always lurking somewhere. Often, when she goes out on foot to run little errands, Clarissa ends up staying out for too long — even for three hours or longer. Sometimes she comes back home with a load of useless things such as sunscreen in the winter, Windex, silver polish, jars of beeswax, Palmolive or a huge quantity of soaps and cleaning products, which are building up in the broom closet and would already be enough for five or six years. A few days ago she came back home with a huge quantity of yogurt that neither of us likes. "There was a special offer," Clarissa said, "and I paid less than half price."

She does all this to show me that she was at the supermarket, the one in Via del Monte della Farina or at the Co-op in Piazza Cavour. She has a thing for supermarkets, Clarissa. When I ask her why she stays out for so long, she'll answer that she was at the supermarket, but most of the time she says that she ran into a friend, and I pretend to believe her. Is it possible that she runs into a friend every time she leaves home? Bah! How is it that when I go out I don't run into anybody? The streets are more or less the same ones that Clarissa walks. Up to the Pantheon on one side, Campo de' Fiori on the other side, Via dei Coronari, Via di Panico, Via Tomacelli, Via della Scrofa and Via del Governo Vecchio, where we live. Clarissa says that I'm absent-minded and that I also have rather blurry vision. Clarissa is such a smart aleck, but as a matter of fact, I am absent-minded, and my prescription does leave much to be desired.

Westerhoff's death would lead me to stop telling the double-headed eagle story, but Clarissa still seems to enjoy it. If I stopped because of the German journalist's death, it would be as if I accused her of a lack of sensitivity.

Could it be possible that Giano is jealous? And yet, what was he doing sitting all alone at the Pantheon café, the one under the Hotel Sole's commemorative stone that reads "Ludovico Ariosto lived here"? From there you can see the office of the urban planning architect, Federico Zandel, a friend of ours whom we often see and who pays me exaggerated compliments in front of Giano all the time — compliments that appear innocent because of their very explicitness. It's a social game that flatters me, but in the long term it ended up bothering Giano. One evening, a journalist from the *Corriere della Sera* had invited us to dinner in the garden of his house in Monte Mario. After dinner, while Giano was reluctantly involved in a political discussion on Iraq, Zandel took my hand and held it for a long time. An innocent sign of love as if between two consummated adulterers.

Ongoing fictions. One day Zandel was accompanying me, arm in arm, up the staircase near the American Academy towards the Gianiculum, while Giano was following a few steps behind, in the company of Zandel's wife — a virtual exchange of respective spouses. Zandel's wife, Irina, however, certainly couldn't spur my jealousy. She is tall and skinny but without curves, and she looks like a lamp post no matter what she wears. Since she is tall and skinny, men say she is beautiful. Giano wanted to court her, at least in reaction to Zandel's courting me, but his metallic voice sounded threatening despite his evident and pathetic disposition to carelessness. She is rich. Everybody agrees on that. She owns stock in a big insurance company. It's a phantom wealth that nobody is able to quantify, but people say it consists of many zeros. It seems that Zandel and Irina live off the interest on the interest. Zandel doesn't worry about this wealth, which his wife manages and which doesn't affect the couple's life in any way.

That day I was wearing a Mochtar Indian silk overcoat, and Zandel praised the fabric for being so sensual to the touch, thinner and softer than velvet. I told him that even the blouse I was wearing was made of the same Indian fabric. He firmly squeezed my arm to tell me he had understood. Our external relationship was shaped by these innocent allusions, which could nonetheless have been a prelude to something. To what? (But when will I stop lying to myself?) Nothing. I am faithful to Giano, even though he sleeps with Valeria (but I am sure, in perfect bad faith, that he doesn't). Frustration and a drowsy suspicion.

Giano is likely to have seated himself in that strategic Pantheon café to check just in case I were to pass by and just in case I were to go to Zandel the architect's office. I spotted him from afar, and I passed by the entrance to Zandel the architect's office without even glancing at it. Then I headed towards Corso Rinascimento to avoid getting too close to the café where Giano was positioned, like a hunter in a barrel for coot hunting. In this case I was the coot. I threw him off the track *en souplesse*, heading with a light pace towards Corso Rinascimento.

This is a strange coincidence. As soon as I find out that Giano secretly met up with Valeria, Giano is spying on me to find out whether I am secretly meeting up with Zandel the architect. Symmetries distress me, but not that much.

GIANO

I'd really like to know why Clarissa takes walks right in front of the entrance to where Zandel the architect has his office. Maybe because she hopes to run into him? Or she just happened to pass by? I don't want to make unkind assumptions. I'm sure she doesn't deserve it. However, I am curious to know why she passed by Zandel's office entrance, which is not on the way from Via del Governo Vecchio, where we live, to Campo de' Fiori, the destination Clarissa announced before going out. Should I convince myself that she just happened to pass by there?

I don't know what she sees in someone like Zandel, with that pale and faded face, which seems to always hide some sort of malice. Wrinkleless face, passionless heart. Clarissa defines it as a postmodern face. What she means by this definition I don't know. Should I worry? If she's committed to this game of fictions then I'll shut up, and we won't say another word about it.

Actually, yesterday I was the stupid one who left Valeria's number on the cordless phone display — what a damn memory this Swatch has! When Clarissa found the recorded number by chance, she asked me whom I had called while she was at the pharmacy. I got away with it by saying that I had spoken with a student, who was doing some research for me on architecture and urban planning in Rome after the Unification, after the Piedmonts' arrival. In keeping with my good rule, I documented my lie with credible detail: a superlative improvisation. Luckily, Clarissa didn't recognize Valeria's number. How could she? However, after finding out that I had told Valeria the double-headed eagle story, Clarissa is in a state of alert, and I have to be more careful.

CLARISSA

I never told Giano that something had happened between me and Zandel twenty-three or twenty-four years ago. I was engaged to Giano, but I had gone on vacation to Porto Santo Stefano together with a little group of friends among whom was Valeria, already known for her Greek nose and her megalomaniac ass even back then. A really greedy person, Valeria. She was alternating between a young architect and a journalist from the *Messaggero*. She ended up sleeping with both. Moreover, Zandel the architect was the owner of the apartment in Via dei Fari where we were staying, and he was very annoyed that Valeria was fucking the journalist from the *Messaggero*. He has a possessive personality, so he felt betrayed by his guest. He was about to kick us out of his place, thus interrupting our vacation. But in the meantime he was persistently coming on to me, and I couldn't resist.

On my part this was a sort of thoughtless goodbye to singlehood, just like men do a few days before they get married. Moreover, I liked the idea of taking a man away from Valeria and at the same time saving our seaside vacation. On that occasion, after we had achieved satisfaction under the sheets, Zandel the architect told me that Valeria was also called "the condo woman" because of her habit of being with more than one man at the same time. I never forgot that definition. In sum, as I knew from experience, she was also a woman to keep at a distance on account of her known quest for married men. By the way, at the end of the vacation, as we said our goodbyes, I was embarrassed because I forgot Zandel's first name, and I owed to him a pleasant, though brief, intimate moment. In my defense I must say that during our brief relationship in those days, I was spontaneously using Zandel's last name as if it were his first name.

I saw him again several years later as my husband's colleague, and who knows whether he still remembered the young lady who, many years earlier in Porto Santo Stefano, et cetera, et cetera? But what the hell am I reminiscing on about? The architect and urban planner Federico Zandel courts me in an empty rhetorical way, and he's never hinted at our distant encounter. He still owns the house in Porto Santo Stefano, and sometimes he invites us there. But he prefers to rent it out every August, and with the six thousand euros from the rent, he chooses a new country for a vacation with his wife, Irina. Sardinia, Corsica, Greece, Turkey, the Red Sea.

Giano doesn't know, but recently, following her old tradition, Valeria has been devoting her attention to younger men, like that professor from La Sapienza, who had asked her to translate an article from German and found himself naked in bed on top of her the same afternoon. News of the event spread around the university, and since that day requests for translations from German have multiplied. And now she was reeling in Giano, or had she already reeled him in? In this unfortunate case, silence to your heart's content.

Yesterday morning at around ten, while I was putting on a scarf to go out, I saw Giano from behind, on the other side of the half-closed bathroom door, leaning toward the sink with his head in his hands. I stopped silently, and I saw that he was sobbing and shaking with tremors that made his shoulders tremble. For a second I thought about calling out to him, then I went away on tiptoe so that he wouldn't realize I was there. I wasn't sure if I was doing the right thing, but my instinct was telling me it was better not to show myself, that perhaps Giano didn't want me to take part in his problems and sorrows, otherwise he would have told me. All the same, I was very surprised by this desperate crying, because it didn't seem to me, as far as I was aware, that Giano had any reason for it, at home or outside.

I had a sudden doubt: what if those heaving shoulders were the result of convulsive laughs? There are identical difficulties of interpretation with crying or laughing, and I was left with an undigested question mark in my stomach. In any case, I could not talk to Giano about it, since he would reproach me for having spied on him, the worst among marital embarrassments. All things considered, I would never solve the dilemma of that sudden and mysterious dissipation of neurons, never ever in my life. But in the end, I said to myself, I won't pull my hair out over this.

LUIGI MALERBA

Clarissa and I were making a list of our acquaintances who had died from AIDS, the new plague of the century, happy to both be exempt from this earthly damnation, which actually strikes our kids' generation most of all. We often play this grim and wide-ranging game with the latest, sad updates; but for some time now our repertoire has included not only that epidemic and the other invasive disease, but also the varied specialties of ailments lethal to humans. We entertain ourselves more than at the movie theater: a few hours of sublime relaxation.

I don't know how it came up, but at a certain point, Clarissa told me that Zandel the architect has only one lung due to a surgery from several years ago. So he, too, is part of this lethal tide.

"How do you know?"

"Somebody told me. I don't remember who. Maybe it was Valeria, the day I ran into her at the French Academy. I believe she also slept with him, or maybe there is still something between them, something bed-related since it involves Valeria. Actually, yes, it was precisely she who told me about Zandel's lung."

It is obvious that Clarissa wanted me to know that there was a relationship going on between Valeria and Zandel. Cold, colder, warmer, hot. I didn't betray my irritation, but I changed the subject because, when Valeria comes up, the subject soon becomes high risk.

But what did Clarissa want to communicate with the news of the amputated lung? That Zandel the architect was not a dangerous competitor? And that he probably has a relationship with Valeria.

"When you see him," I replied, "he's bursting with good health."

"Actually, he's as yellow as a lemon."

"Okay, he's pale, but that's his natural complexion. It doesn't mean anything."

"If he's only got one lung, it must mean something. You can't see it from the outside, but it means he's only half breathing."

"I can't have sympathy. He works a lot abroad on the layout of roads and sidewalks in historic cities. He's fixed sidewalks in Amsterdam, Hamburg, Cologne and Zurich. When he presented his project for the rebuilding of the historic city center of Rome, his colleagues laughed, and yet it seems like the city council will entrust him with an initial parcel of sidewalks for the area from Piazza del Popolo up to Via Condotti and Via di Ripetta. The most elegant area in Rome, a gold mine.

"When Rome's city council renovated the pavement and the sidewalks from Largo Argentina up to Piazza di Pietra for the Holy Year, they consulted Zandel, who suggested importing the basalt sheets and the cobblestones from China, where they cost a tenth of the Italian price. At the city council they were perplexed, because the Holy Year pilgrims would have to walk on communist pavement. In the end the price, convenience and quality of the Chinese manufacturing prevailed.

"In conclusion Zandel has become an international specialist in sidewalks, and it seems that the object of his ultimate ambition is New York. Sidewalks as the last resort of a lost and depressed humanity. Walking, taking a walk. Sidewalk as a metaphor, a metaphor on which Zandel walks triumphant with his wallet stuffed with thousands and thousands of euros."

"You are making fun of your colleague and friend."

"Not really. Sidewalks contribute to the respectability of a city. They allow city dwellers not only to walk, but also to take walks and to think while they take a walk, just like the Peripatetic philosophers of ancient Greece. And above all they provide Zandel with shiny, jingling euros, just like Pinocchio's coins. And this is good. Because money is good. Moreover, he's got a very rich wife."

"Are you reproaching me because I'm not rich?"

I hugged Clarissa to make up for the accidental slip.

"Despite his cloven lung, it seems that Zandel has a lot of lovers," I said.

This was a low blow. Clarissa clammed up. Her curiosity was ready to burst, but she contained herself. She didn't ask me any questions. Well done.

CLARISSA

I don't know where Giano fishes up some of his news. Does he make it up? I didn't bat an eyelash at the news about Zandel's numerous lovers. What if it were true? What if every time Zandel can't see me due to his work appointments — so he says — he were actually in the little room next to his office fucking some lady who's been let out on leave? The secretary is his accomplice when it is me in that little room — there, I said it — but by the same token, when it's me calling, she could answer the phone discretely and say that Zandel the architect is out. And what is his stupid wife doing? Is she sleeping? She is beautiful — so they say, but I find her to be a piece of wood — rich, and an idiot. But I can't complain. Would it be convenient for me if she were smart and wily? The important thing is that Zandel goes on courting me when we see each other with Giano: a displayed fiction to hide the truth. And I will continue to play the game of courtship, joking around and pretending I'm flattered. In a week we will have three days all to ourselves, because Giano is going to Strasbourg to a conference on "The City of the Future."

Giano has always paid close attention to the poisons of the world. Even jealousy is a poison, but there are worse. He was wracked with convulsions when the United States refused to ratify the Kyoto Protocol. Cursing, invectives, cursing. Ever since then Giano has refused all American drinks and has eliminated Kellogg's Corn Flakes from his breakfast, as they're made with GMO corn.

After the soldiers who had been in contact with depleted uranium munitions became sick, the Americans, with unpunished arrogance, made it known that they had used depleted uranium munitions in Iraq, too. Well done, Giano says. And they had to admit through clenched teeth that they used white phosphorus bombs on Falluja after testimony by some marines and the images on TV of the carbonized bodies. Very well done. Moreover, they happily go on producing spray cans, a gracious contribution to the destruction of the sky.

During his sleep Giano mutters strange and obscene curses about the hole in the ozone layer.

GIANO

At the conference on "The City of the Future," everybody was expecting me to talk about Urban Deconstruction, but instead I spoke enthusiastically about the idea of a city shaped like a star, where the points are inhabited and the empty parts between one point and the next are occupied by gardens. Circular connecting streets pass systematically through the inhabited areas and the parks. The Great Ring Road of Rome, the Ring in Vienna, the four concentric street rings in Beijing, these are mere remedies for cities built according to traditional criteria. The City of the Future will be shaped like a star from the start, no matter whether it's the Star of David with six points or that of Salomon with five points or the Rose of the Wind with eight or any other number of points. In any event the points will be connected by concentric rings joined to one another by radial streets. The rings would border the various urban areas. Each connecting street will be one-way, alternating from the center towards the exterior or from the exterior towards the center. Numerous small irregularities will be planned to prevent urban boredom, which always waits in ambush. A mistake here and there is good for the health of the world. The subway will cross the city in the four cardinal directions, and it will be elevated, with panoramic views and on a single rail just like the one at Disneyland in Los Angeles.

The future is a long way down the road — I added — and so, in the meantime, we can correct traditional cities by gradually realizing innovations. In conclusion we will have to bear in mind the big picture and carry out smaller projects in the interim. I completed my talk with a note on wind, which is important to keep in mind when determining the height, the inclination and the shape of the buildings. Thus you can avoid repeating the resounding mistake made in Rome, in the aftermath of the war, when the buildings in the EUR neighborhood were constructed too tall and so blocked the way of a refreshing wind, called the Ponentino, that comes from the sea. As a result, they changed the climate of the Capital for the worse, and in the historic center they created stagnant pockets of poisons, such as carbon dioxide and lethal PM_{10}s. You are standing there, mesmerized in front of the Pantheon, and they silently creep into your lungs.

It is easier to realize my project in Africa, where cities are often shapeless conglomerations of shacks that are just waiting to be demolished and redone according to rational criteria. Or in China, where cities are invented from nothing. A chapter on energy: in the same way that electric energy and gas are provided, in the City of the Future, a big central plant will provide hot water to the whole urban area, just like a huge gas water heater. Each apartment will be able to connect to the hot water distribution pipes the same way it's connected to gas or electricity.

Right there on the spot, my talk triggered a round of applause, though a good part of it was improvised based on notes I had brought from Rome. But during the discussion period, a young Russian urban planner intervened to compliment me, because he had now learned that the future is a long way down the road — is tomorrow also a long way down the road, by chance? — and, above all, because I had reinvented the wheel, since in Moscow there already is a single plant that provides hot water to every house, just like I had proposed in my model for the City of the Future.

Put on the spot, I remained speechless. Why was I uninformed about this important work in Moscow? I had been in that city only once, and it seemed to me that, in Italy, we had nothing to learn from Muscovite urban planning. I answered the colleague who had made me the butt of his joke by saying that I would certainly leave the Russians the record for reinventing the wheel and that I was aware of other records of theirs, such as the Stalinist roads in Moscow that were two or three hundred meters wide but sadly lacked any intersecting trams or buses allowing citizens to cross them.

The bickering went on for a while, and according to many delegates that was the most brilliant part of the conference, though it was the most vulgar according to me. The Russian delegate's comment was vulgar, and my retort was equally vulgar. Even now I can't make sense of how I let myself be dragged so low, into an abyss of vulgarity. Yet this was the despicable level of the renowned urban planners who came to Strasbourg from all over the planet.

During dinner with a small group of presenters, I conversed politely even with the ironic Russian delegate, and all was proceeding smoothly until a surly Italian deputy with a beard shaped like a double-headed ax decided to join us. As he sat down at the table I stood up, suddenly manifesting symptoms of allergic intolerance. Some presenters who had understood what kind of allergy was at the root of my flight imitated me, and they too left the table.

It's not the first time I've suffered from such para-political distresses. It is a real disease that I even told my doctor about, and he prescribed me two Laroxyl pills a day and an antidepressant that, however, did nothing to me, neither good nor bad. Well, my doctor said, what has to be eliminated is the cause. As if more than half of all Italians were not interested in such an enterprise! He also said that, in the long run, my anguishing political allergies could provoke a gastric ulcer, and he was already treating some cases of that. In conclusion, he explained to me that I was ill with a "dormant ulcer," a paradoxical situation that prefers to afflict subjects who somaticize serious problems of the day.

After dinner with the presenters and after I fled from the restaurant, I walked toward my hotel, the small Hotel Cathédrale in Strasbourg's pedestrian center, just in front of Notre-Dame Cathedral. In the double room I had booked from Rome, I found Valeria, who had arrived by train in the afternoon as agreed. I couldn't hide my bad mood over what had happened at the conference and then at the restaurant. When I told her about the bickering in which I had been involved, she found it funny. I forgave her for her lack of sensitivity, like that of the eminent urban planners at the conference, who had applauded us. I didn't reprimand her so as not to spoil our meeting, which was safely taking place far away from our coordinates in Rome. I never talk to Valeria about my anguishing political allergies, a topic that I dump all on Clarissa. She can bear any complaint, because to a certain degree she also considers my illness imaginary. Unfortunately she doesn't realize that often people with imaginary illnesses die from the illness they imagined.

I hope I didn't disappoint Valeria the night we spent together. The meeting in the small Hotel Cathédrale, all boiserie, brocades and upholstered walls, with a strange, almost brothel-like atmosphere, should have triggered my aggression, which had been humiliated at the conference. Instead, it was the normal, warm, time-tested amatory routine.

"Imagine the boredom of living in a small and taciturn city like this."

"I could finally keep the windows open. How marvelous," Valeria said.

"I prefer Rome even with closed windows."

"The past few days in Rome the heat has been suffocating. September is the hottest month of the year."

"July is also the hottest month of the year, and August as well."

Valeria nodded with a smile. Every attempt to converse with Valeria plummets into a delicious and relaxing universal collection of stupidity.

In the streets around the area, while we were looking for a café for breakfast in place of the hotel's sad dining room, we walked the full length of a flower market on Place du Château: a triumph of colors and scents. I gave Valeria a bunch of cyclamens, which are not too encumbering but very scented. Our walk was almost silent. Despite her libertine life, which, after all, she doesn't hide, Valeria's mere presence was enough to erase the residue of the past, which often weighs down the mood of many ladies and young ladies who haven't managed to create a solid romantic life for themselves. It was a stroll during which we were happy to be together there in Strasbourg, although we were both somehow curt, myself more so than she. I felt serene and tranquil, even somewhat stupid. The miracles of geography: there in Strasbourg under a lead sky so mysterious and enchanting, I saw Valeria with naïve eyes. All was new around us.

Thinking back today on that sort of happiness, suspended in emptiness, the memory of a parallel feeling appears, a feeling experienced with Clarissa during a trip to New York. We were strolling around the cold, brisk streets like two dumb tourists, without even half an idea in our heads, happy to be there together in that city with no need to talk, our presence being enough for one another. Strange how similar situations and feelings repeat themselves in two different places — Strasbourg and New York — and above all with two very different people like Clarissa and Valeria. The difference is that in New York Clarissa and I saw a rainbow.

Even feelings repeat themselves, I said to myself, just like the alternation of seasons, and we accept such repetitions in nature without protest. So many springs, so many summers, so many falls, so many winters, and again from the beginning. So many dawns and so many dusks.

Giano left a large notebook on the table. A black marker had traced two letters on it: U.D. They were initials as gloomy and harsh as a pair of gravediggers. It is clear that they stand for Urban Deconstruction, and tempted though I might be to read the text to know a little bit more about Giano's projects, as soon as I opened the notebook I shut it right away, because I really didn't want to disrespect him by sticking my nose into one of his private realms. Besides, Giano's handwriting is so dense and difficult to read that it would be a struggle, and what for? Curiosity? I admit that I am curious to finally read about my husband's projects and theories.

During our first year of marriage, I used to suffer a great deal because I didn't know much about Giano's urban planning, which, by the way, attracted a lot of interest even outside the university. Every now and then somebody would try to befriend me, hoping to discover who-knows-what secrets that would explain so radical a theory of urban planning as his. Little by little I got used to avoiding their questions, and it is too late to change my attitude, even if I now have a chance to learn all about Urban Deconstruction, just lying there on the table. In the end it's me asking for information from the students who now and then come to consult some book in Giano's library.

Since Giano started filling up pages and pages with his illegible handwriting, his detachment from reality and his absence have been worsening with each passing day. I have tried to ask him in passing some questions about this project, which occupies him for two or three hours every day. I thought that in the end my interest would please him, but from his evasive answers I understood that I'm not supposed to distract his concentration, which is essential to his writing.

Zandel thinks that Giano, overpowered by complex and discordant thoughts, hopes to find some point of connection between his ideas for urban planning and Heidegger's philosophy, which has recently become quite fashionable and is at the center of all his reflections. "God laughs when men think," Zandel added, quoting the Bible. Good luck with that. But now, please, don't think that I'm being ironic about my husband. I'm only quoting Zandel who was quoting the Bible.

Every now and then I would think back to his relationship with Valeria, which I discovered thanks to the joke about the two-headed eagle. But then, I told myself, a person like Giano, who is completely devoted to dialectics and paradox, could hardly have a relationship with a shallow and mundane woman like Valeria. She's a libertine by vocation and perhaps by calculation, an expert slut. Giano is incomprehensible.

Even eroticism must require some common interests and ideas. What? Is Valeria, with her big ass, capable of having interests or ideas? Giano is incomprehensible.

GIANO

In Valle Giulia I ran into Morpurgo the architect, who had given a talk in the main auditorium on the use of urban spaces in the modern architecture of Tokyo. It was more or less a repetition of his talk from the conference on the City of the Future in Strasbourg. I said hello and reiterated my compliments on his talk. I started chatting him up because, based on things Valeria said on her return trip, I was suspicious.

When I asked him how his return from Strasbourg had gone, his face brightened as he answered, "Fantastic!"

He then satisfied my curiosity by telling me all the details of his meeting with a young woman on the sleeper car. I immediately identified her: it was Valeria.

Morpurgo is a likable man, and it is easy to see why his sleeper car companion would have liked him. I recognized the truth of his adventure from a few distinctive traits Morpurgo mentioned, such as her sensual habit of sticking her tongue in her partner's ears, a sort of personal signature of Valeria's.

"And you didn't ask to see her again in Rome?"

"God forbid, I am a married man with a jealous wife, and even the woman from the sleeper car is married or almost, from what I understood. Or at least in a stable relationship."

I expected myself to have a jealous breakdown, but nothing happened. I understood that I have to take Valeria for what she is: a woman capable of having two parallel affairs or, as in this case, willing to gladly allow herself the luxury of a night of love with Morpurgo the architect, well aware that everything would start and end right there, in the narrow bed of a sleeper car.

I'm not jealous, but I feel a certain bothersome itch. I asked myself whether my reaction was normal or whether I was once again running along the edge of a cliff. This is what my friend had said to me one day, trying to push me onto the therapist's couch. Never, ever. Psychoanalysis is the disease for which it is believed to be the therapy, I told him, quoting a famous aphorism by Karl Kraus. Anyhow, I decided I wouldn't mention her adventure when I talked to Valeria. It seems that the *ta-ta-tum ta-ta-tum* of a train in motion is a powerful aphrodisiac, but this does not justify Valeria's behavior. Or does it? Thank God I'm not jealous otherwise I would have to slap her, or even worse, in a dramatic

LUIGI MALERBA

gesture, attack her like jealous lovers do, something you can read about in the newspapers. Kitchen knives are very fashionable.

The world spins, and excessive things happen. I take note of these reflections because I've decided that one of these days I will organize them into a book. I already have many pages of notes written, like the text of a novel. No knives.

I wasn't able to understand Giano's mood when he came back from Strasbourg. He's been home for a week, and I am still waiting for a report about his trip. Conferences usually provide a topic of conversation for at least a few days, unlike the theories of Deconstruction he develops for his university classes, which are excluded from our household life. But in fact, there was no report. If anything, he was in a bad mood, as if his participation had gone poorly. However, Tiberio Morpurgo, a colleague of his at the university who was also there in Strasbourg, says that Giano was brilliant and well applauded. So what's the reason for his bad mood?

I can do nothing but stop him from reading the newspaper. With every piece of bad news — and this shoddily put-together Italy provides us with one a day — Giano suffers a crisis of sadness, heartburn (Pepto-Bismol), insomnia, allergic asthma. He wakes up at night, sits on the bed and complains about his helplessness in the face of all the world's disasters and especially those in Italy. "What can I do?" he asks me. Nothing really, poor Giano, besides waking me up at 4 in the night. Or should I say in the morning? So he throws up his hands, as if these misfortunes were directed against him, even though they take place not only in Italy but in Iraq, Pakistan, Iran, India, China, the Mediterranean, the United States. His is a global frustration.

Poor Giano, I was trying to console him: "There's nothing we can do about it. We are all on the same Titanic."

I wish I had never mentioned that unfortunate Titanic. "We're sinking," said Giano, who can't swim and is scared as fuck of the water. It was the genuine hysterical crisis of a man about to drown. I was frightened because he was short of breath, as if he were really under water. He tossed himself out of the bed, holding on to a small table as if it were a shard of a shipwreck to avoid going to the bottom. His face was dripping with sweat, his eyes wide open in fright, and his hands were shaking. I wanted to give him a tranquilizer, but he had exploded at other times in the past and once had thrown the packet of Laroxyl out the window.

If his students were to see him.

Finally he sat on the couch and, little by little, as still as a fakir, he silently reacquired his precarious, cataleptic normality. After about ten minutes, he woke up once more. He dragged me to the couch and wanted to make love with great ardor and fierce energy. Fortunately, the maid was sleeping and so didn't rush to my aid, as had happened once a few months before, when she heard my moaning in the living room. It happens that I emit very sharp screams when I make love. Zandel had double windows and a padded door installed in the room next to his office.

It is obvious that Giano's sexual outbursts compensate for his dramatic, global frustration. After each of these cyclical, hysterical crises, Giano performs in bed with such ardor and vigor that he gets me off three or even four times in a row. Unfortunately, it happens very rarely because Giano always tries to avoid political conversations, whereas I haven't done anything to avoid them for quite a while. I only intervene when the crisis is already underway, well aware that it's too late. In fact, the emotional breakdown follows a rough and repetitive course. I have no arguments to oppose to his breakdowns (as a parenthesis, I agree with Giano, although I control my reactions), and when Giano has completely melted down, I reap the benefits that evening in bed.

I'm sure that Valeria reaps them, too, some afternoons. Certain evenings Giano comes home exhausted and with a stomach ache. I know where he spent his afternoon, but I pretend to believe he's got a stomach ache and that's it. Well, that's not really it.

"Why on earth did they ban Alka-Seltzer?" Giano complains to make his distress more believable. Now you tell me what I can do with such a husband. The bad part is that I love him. Very much, like an idiot.

GIANO

It's been raining for fifteen days. A swirling wind knocked down three pine trees on Lungotevere Matteotti, an enormous cedar from Lebanon at Villa Celimontana, a Roman holm oak in Piazza Mazzini and unroofed a warehouse in Forte Boccea. The German pope said that the wind symbolizes the Holy Spirit. Oh my! So was the Holy Spirit pissed off at the Capital? Every fall Rome turns into a huge puddle. These streets around Piazza Navona are all lower than the Tiber, and one day I expect to find the street flooded with water and end up trapped at home until firemen finally arrive with rafts. I'm exaggerating, of course. It's just this authoritarian imagination of mine that chases me when it rains.

Next summer I want to see if Clarissa will once again suggest we go to Porto Santo Stefano, where Zandel has a house and a boat. Between you and me, I get mortally bored at the seaside, whereas Clarissa is crazy about it. Together with Zandel's wife, she sunbathes naked on the boat while I sit around scratching my balls. Along with other things, there in Porto Santo Stefano it's impossible to get any peace because once a day Zandel suggests going on a trip to Sardinia or to Corsica or at least to Giglio Island. This is a real misfortune for someone like me, who goes to the seaside to be left alone, to read a few books in the shade — when it's hot I look for shade, not for the sun — or to take long naps while breathing the iodized sea air. The only reason I ever agree to go out in Zandel's boat is my yearning to make him fall into the water, far away from the coast, by accident of course.

Zandel's passion for sailing is strange, because each time he goes out to sea in his boat he turns on the auxiliary engine and uses that to keep going. In short, I bet he doesn't know how to make the sails work, not even for a short jaunt on the open sea.

I have to admit that his boat is beautiful. It's varnished in blue, and everybody admires it even when it's anchored at the Porto Vecchio. Meanwhile Zandel is sitting at the Café Chiodo to keep an eye on it like a treasure. Relax, it won't run away. It was christened with the name *Irina*, in full display, written in capital letters and in a nice art deco cursive. It's an homage to his wife and her money, which bought and pays for the up-keep of his wonderful toy.

The first time I dared to openly oppose Zandel was when he suggested going to Corsica for the hundredth time, to the eastern coast of the island, to a nudist village about which he had been told marvels. Who knows what kind of marvels, if not just seeing a bunch of naked women? Clearly Zandel had already been there because he told us too much detail about how the nudists take off their clothes: not only on the beach, but they often go strolling to the café completely naked. He also told us the story of a young lady who tried to get into the pool wearing an almost invisible bottom and was forced by the lifeguard to fucking take that off too.

The strange thing is that Clarissa didn't seem shocked at all by the story, to the point that I wondered whether she had already heard it by chance or whether she had even been there too. In June she had gone to Corsica with a friend while I was busy with exams in Valle Giulia. Probably not, I said to myself. It was just that she wanted to appear nonchalant, and, perhaps, she hoped to convince me to agree to Zandel's proposal. He had been more shameless than ever, since he said, just as a joke, that after all Clarissa could go to Corsica with him and Irina while I was busy at the university. Clarissa laughed, but she didn't say no. Though I didn't show it, I was furious, more at Clarissa's attitude than at Zandel's proposal, which I opposed with a smile on my lips but my balls in flames. It wasn't about the usual courtship, which was now a routine, but about a real attack against our marital peace. All naked there in Corsica. In moments like these I'm seized by a roguish anger at my wife, a storm of neurons that I can barely control. Luckily it lasts only a few minutes, but these are explosive minutes that are more dangerous the more I struggle to bottle them up.

Every evening and sometimes even at the university, during the brief intermissions between one class and another, I have started to write in a big notebook a novel with four protagonists: Clarissa, Zandel, Valeria and me. Obviously with fictional names: Marozia, Zurlo, Bubi and Tania. I had thought about calling myself Gaio[1] instead of Bubi, but the anagram, although imperfect, was too overt. And gaiety is not really a personal peculiarity of mine and therefore not part of the character who corresponds to me either. No gaiety for Giano.

It's a bourgeois novel, just like its protagonists. But more than a novel, it's an escape from my bottled-up anger. On the cover of the notebook I put only two initials, U.D., which stand for Urban Deconstruction. Since I almost always leave the notebook at home, where I never keep anything locked up, I'm sure that these initials and my terrible handwriting will be enough to dissuade Clarissa from reading it.

CLARISSA

I don't know why Zandel goes on with his increasingly risqué provocations, which verge on the obscene, and why he is getting such a kick out of embarrassing me. He compared me to a turtle, and everybody knows that turtles are lascivious, and they scream loudly during their long fuck sessions. As for that discussion of nudists and the story of the topless young lady who wanted to get into the pool and was forced to get naked by the lifeguard, luckily it was difficult to figure out that the young lady was me. Zandel wanted to flatter me with the description of the young lady's fantastic beauty. He had started the story as if a third party had told it to him, but it was very clear that, in reality, he himself had witnessed the event. Later on, when he began describing the way her bush was parted, I felt like I was being stripped right there, in front of two men who had seen me naked many times. But this was not supposed to happen: them, seeing me naked together, at the same time, even if only imagining it with their eyes.

Zandel was dwelling on his description of how my curly bush was parted, and then he said something he shouldn't have said, namely, that the bush was blond while the young lady's hair was dark. I was already feeling uncomfortable with having being stripped and described in such detail, but when Zandel mentioned her blond pubic hair and the dark hair on her head, I sank through the floor. In fact that difference, almost a contradiction, belonged to my body, and Giano could have easily understood that, by talking about the naked young lady, Zandel was actually talking about Clarissa, present, right there.

At that point I really thought it was time to intervene.

"It's quite normal," I said, "for pubic hair to be a different color from the head, the same way a dark-haired man's beard can be blond. If you are surprised," I added out of spite against Zandel, "it just means that you don't have much experience with women."

I smiled to imply that I could talk because I knew better, and I said one more time that the difference was not that strange because a friend of mine also had it: a blond pussy and dark hair.

After telling the story Zandel apologized, joking around — yet another provocation — for having suggested going to Corsica among the nudists to Giano, who — as he well knew — was extremely prudish. But instead of saying prudish he said *priggish* with seemingly innocent irony. And he resumed the story of the young lady made to undress by the lifeguard so that he could say something that hit me in the viscera, as the ancients would say. In the stomach, I say.

"It might sound strange," Zandel said in a different voice, which was now serious and deep, "but that young lady has remained imprinted in my eyes and burned in my heart. I swear that the image of her naked has nothing to do with this thought. So I looked her in the eyes. Our gazes crossed, and I immediately realized that I could love that young lady and that if I hadn't been married, I could have even found in her a partner through the end of my days. These are the kinds of thing that one realizes one day, all of a sudden. It's what people call love at first sight, right there, by the poolside in a nudist village in eastern Corsica."

"Wait, didn't you say that someone who was there in the nudist village had told you the story?"

"I lied. Is that against the law?"

"It's not against the law, but it's pointless. And at your age, it would have been unworkable to enter into a marriage-like relationship with a young lady more or less in her twenties, if I understood your story correctly."

Twenty years old! This was an almost imperceptible moment of embarrassment for me as if confronted with a new lie.

Zandel had recounted his story with a tone of voice that I recognized, one that he saves for those most rare and special occasions, or rather, for important speeches that take up his entire persona. I've already said this, but I felt involved in his words with all my senses and feelings, and I realized that our relationship was not just a matter of getting along and having sex, instead, it combined our two persons in a warm whirlpool of love. Right there, I suddenly discovered I was in love with Zandel, who up until that moment was only a secret and amorous partner of mine. A sublime rarity: his words were a real, true declaration of love, made in the presence of Giano, who had thrown me a life jacket by ascribing the age of twenty to the forty-year-old, topless young lady.

All of a sudden, the love between me and Zandel appeared to me in a completely new light. I could feel the burst of flames on my face and in flashes all over my body. It was a silent joy, which later developed into daring images before I fell asleep each night with the light musical background of Coleman Hawkins's sax. Perhaps these were also the flames of betrayal, which in an extreme paradox were rekindling my love for Giano. In a way, it's a therapeutic betrayal. And now I beg you not to think that this is all a hypocritical invention of mine to justify my adultery.

I can now say, I can swear, that I didn't know I was in love with Zandel. I swear it with shame. Am I so stupid, I said to myself, that I didn't realize I was in love? Up to this day I still haven't understood why I am like this, so completely stupid. We were sitting on the terrace of our house, looking at the view of the dome of Sant'Andrea della Valle, and question marks were flying around me like those seagulls sailing in the sky, illuminated from below by the lights of the city.

It seemed to me that Giano was slightly annoyed by Zandel's story. Could it be, perhaps, that he remembered I had taken a trip to Corsica last June? Was he then slightly annoyed because he was suspicious of our mutual friend's feelings, even though they were supposedly directed toward a stranger? Was it really a stranger? After Zandel left, Giano didn't say anything else about Corsica and the nudists. In sum, he wanted me to believe that Zandel's provocations passed by without leaving a trace. Better this way, I said to myself, better if he walls up his jealousy with a solid concrete barrier so that it doesn't overflow.

We remained on the terrace for another half an hour to silently admire the beautiful Roman darkness dotted only with bright seagulls.

GIANO

As if I hadn't understood that last summer Clarissa went with Zandel to Corsica, to the nudist village, and that the topless young lady who wanted to dive into the pool could have been precisely her, Clarissa, in person. Even though, since Clarissa is forty, Zandel's compliments seemed to be a bit exaggerated. It's obvious. They had agreed not to reveal that they had gone to the nudist village together. In fact, Zandel told the story of the topless young lady who wanted to dive into the pool as if it were a second-hand story. Then he lost control of the narration and betrayed himself. He admitted that he had witnessed the event. I just don't understand where his wife was. Clearly she was not in Corsica at the nudist village too.

Completely naked. Between you and me I can understand the desire to see Clarissa naked in public. Was it innocent voyeurism? I wish it were only that. And what about that solemn declaration of love? Perhaps my presence was making the game more exciting? Try and figure out the reasoning of a fanatic and fanciful erotomaniac like Zandel. Goodbye, Kamasutra!

I can already see them: her on the bottom and him on top, oxygen deprived. For an instant I'm able to erase the image with a screen of fog created by my despair, but suddenly those two reappear: him on top, actually no, they switched positions and now he is on the bottom and she's on top to delay orgasm and prolong their intercourse. I can already see them, just like that, completely naked night and day, in the midst of a small crowd of men and women who are completely naked, strolling around the nudist village among centuries-old olive trees with trunks carved like ancient sculptures. Who would ever raise his eyes to look at the sky when there is such an abundance of legs and bushes to see, the bushes often purposely ruffled as if they had just come out of a fashionable salon or an erotic battle. That's why Clarissa never told me about the nudist village. No wonder. Why would she hide her (probable) trip among the nudists? Because you go there to get laid. It's written all over the place.

Here in my eyes the image of those two reappears while they toss and turn in bed. I must have some nerve when I say I'm not jealous of Clarissa. I am willing to put up with the thirst and the sand of the desert in order to forget about that whore, Clarissa, in bed with the infamous Zandel, who has only one lung.

What can I do about my shitty life? Nothing. Nothing because I can't live without Clarissa, who for her part, I have now understood, can't live without Zandel. It's a situation with no way out. And so what future is there for this poor urban planner and unhappy architect? Please, let there be a little bit of future for him too.

CLARISSA

Giano spends every evening filling his notebook on Urban Deconstruction with his dense handwriting. No more television at night — I agree — but when he's tired of writing he immerses himself in reading *Don Quixote,* not Heidegger, as Zandel insinuated. Apparently reading this big book provides him with the tension he needs to compose his treatise.

With difficulty, and skipping a few words, I managed to read the opening pages of the book that has the two initials of Urban Deconstruction as a title on the cover. I immediately figured out that something was off. And now here I am, overcome with surprise. What shocked me right off the bat was that Giano's text begins with the little story of the double-headed eagle. The eagle's nest is on a tall rocky wall, and that fucking eagle with two heads flies up to it, exactly the same as Giano has told it a hundred times. It's strange, I said to myself, to begin a book on Urban Deconstruction with the little imperial story he heard from poor Johannes who died on the road in Frankfurt. With difficulty, I read a few more pages, and I realized that the book has nothing whatsoever to do with the Urban Deconstruction referenced on its cover. It's a misleading title, probably to dissuade me from the idea of snooping around in his notebook. A childish ruse, which did work for a little while, though.

What is it about, then? I got an idea by reading a few more pages, with difficulty: my first thought was that it's not a journal, but a long story or even a novel actually. And Giano doesn't want anybody to know about it; or rather, he doesn't want me to know. As if writing a novel were something shameful. But what about a novel that begins with the little story of the double-headed eagle? How can you begin a novel like that? It's obvious that Giano wants to come off as nonchalant, the typical attitude of an amateur.

Giano goes on with his writing, which I decoded with great difficulty and a few gaps. In the narration, it is revealed that, because of the little story, Marozia — who clearly stands for Clarissa — the wife of Giano — called Bubi in the book — finds out that her husband is secretly seeing Tania (Valeria), a lascivious and unscrupulous woman — Tania rhymes with nymphomania: intentional? What's strange is that, according to the book, Marozia — Clarissa is supposed to have found out about the affair between Bubi and Tania, but she put up with it in silence because she also had a relationship outside her marital home, I mean bed. She was with Zurlo, a ridiculous name that came out of Giano's poisoned pen and clearly stands for Zandel. Zurlo is a ridiculous name for a person, but I have to say that Bubi is more suitable for a dog than for an urban-planning architect like Giano.

This novel is clearly the revenge of its author who understood that by manipulating appearances he is able to choreograph a tarantella full of erotic and adulterous futilities. Is this supposed to be his version of the Bourgeois Novel, which at a certain point he suggests as a title? And are these the protagonists? All ghosts, Roman ghosts in this valley of gossip. Is this his idea of our society — let's even call it bourgeois — composed of dull sexual encounters and jokes? In any case, reality has its discretion and its dignity, but if it's transposed onto paper it often becomes unbearable. Judging from the few pages I was able to read, more than a portrait of our bourgeois society this book is the portrait of its author, Giano, and his distorted and wretched perspective. Sure, I feel bad, but I am talking precisely about my husband.

These few pages were enough for me to decide that I will never again open this dishonest notebook. I am already regretting having opened it once.

GIANO

So many bad thoughts cross my mind when I think of Corsica. May Zandel be struck by every curse in the world. May he sink in an African swamp full of mosquitoes and hornets. May he be bitten on his nose by a rattlesnake. May a gigantic hippo shit on his head! I get lost in such images, and in the end I realize that my thoughts head in a malicious direction: the unmentionable desire that Zandel come to a bad end. It's a secret thought. I even wrote a commemoration, thinking they would ask me for one when he dies. In the newspapers' editorial offices they call it a "pre-obit," and they have it ready for the very old or the very sick. The only thing is that with the poison I feel inside, I've already written more than thirty pages about his alleged death. I highly recommend them to you as a pre-obit: dead people are very demanding, and one must always praise them, but my pages don't include even ten lines of positive judgment. And so I'll see about adding some of these pages here and there in my novel.

In a modern novel you can fit in a little bit of everything. I even thought I would include an episode from the Gospel according to John, when the merchant follows Jesus and begs him to heal his son, left at home on the verge of death. Jesus has him beg for a while, then in the end tells the merchant to return home where he will find his son healed. The man goes home and really does find his son once again in perfect health. But all of a sudden, he has a doubt and asks his wife at what time the boy got up from bed. It's the same time when Jesus told him his son would be healed. Good. The merchant, who is suspicious like all merchants, is now satisfied, and he sets his mind to rest. I don't see how I can make use of this episode from the Gospel, but since I've already written it, I'm going to leave it there, nailed to the page. Then I will decide whether to cut it or somehow adapt it to one of my characters. For instance, to Zurlo, who is dying and is miraculously saved by my writing. Me in place of Jesus.

Since when? I shiver, but I don't give up. If Zandel succumbs because of the snake's poison, if he doesn't endure the curse of the swamp or if he dies suffocated by the hippo's shit, it will be the snake's fault, which is a natural creature just like a hippo, a mosquito or an African swamp hornet. I mean, I didn't invent the rattlesnake. It wasn't me who invented the African swamp with malaria-carrying mosquitoes and hornets. What do I have to do with all that? And if Zurlo does die, then what does it matter?

Unfortunately the fact still remains that I wished for his death, but a wish is not enough to make him die. How many men wish for another man's death ? Such a large number that if these wishes came true, world overpopulation would be curbed. The most important thing is that I don't stab him or shoot him in the head to satisfy my wish. In other words, I'm not a murderer, and I don't have any true vocation for killing. To be absolutely clear, my desires are merely virtual and seedy, since they don't lead to anything and only manage to attain a bit of satisfaction from my pages.

It's a bourgeois novel. Its characters, despite everything, belong to the human race, and I prefer to let them die a natural death.

CLARISSA

That day in Corsica Zandel knew that I would have liked to go back to our bungalow instead of taking my topless swimsuit off and jumping in the pool, but in the end I obeyed the lifeguard who was there to impose the rules of the tribe on me, too. So I dove in right away to blow off the steam of my embarrassment, but also to avoid pleasing those who were looking at me the way you look at someone who is ashamed and trying to use her hands to hide her bush. They might ask, what is someone like me doing in a nudist village anyway?

Zandel was playing a wicked game, since with that story he had managed to arouse Giano through the presence of a beautiful, naked female stranger, who was actually his wife. Giano could have never imagined that Zandel was talking about Clarissa, who was right there in front of him, pretending to be bored. On the other hand, what if he understood everything? I must say that Giano switches between profound naivety and brilliant insights. Zandel specialized in paying me compliments that verged on the limits of decency, but he always did so with a great deal of elegance and irony in front of Giano, who accepted it as a frivolous game, perhaps with a certain pride, because his wife was so popular. It was as if these compliments, paid in broad daylight, were an insurance policy against adultery.

It's clear that Zandel was taking satisfaction in these narrative displays. And now, protected by the alibi of anonymity, he was inflating his praises of the young lady's body: beautiful and sensual like a Greek statue. At this point, Giano intervened and explained with sound pedantry that in reality the ancient Greeks admired above all the beauty of the male body and not female nudes. In fact in classical sculpture, it is men who nearly always appear naked, like the Riace bronzes, while women are always amply draped. The only exceptions are the goddesses, naked at last, just like the men.

For my part, I had to consider that I was past forty, and those praises, which I welcomed with silent gratitude, were perhaps somewhat exaggerated. And they completely befuddled Giano, who could not have imagined that I was the young lady, the beautiful forty-year-old young lady.

Luckily men don't look at knees and hands, which are the two categorical clues that betray one's age. Take a look at women's hands and, when they're uncovered, their knees. Most of the time you'll see that their skin is as wrinkled as a turtle's. But at least turtles, wrinkle by wrinkle, hack it till they're two hundred years old. For women, hands and knees should be given a lift, even before the face.

Forget that. I can easily show off not only my knees but even my tits, my ass and my belly button.

GIANO

Whenever I go to her place, which is nearly always in the afternoon, Valeria offers me a coffee or a tea, depending on the time. I hope that the tea — it's always mint tea, unfortunately — helps me neutralize the poison I absorb during my walk up to Via Properzio where she lives, right in front of a device that the city council installed to measure carbon monoxide and lethal particulate matter in the air. Most of the time I walk by without looking at that device, which dispenses apprehension.

Valeria doesn't hide her libertine past. It's not clear whether she's ever fallen in love in her life. I don't know of even a single important love story, which every woman has in her account of the past. Anyhow a love that could be called romantic is never part of Valeria's stories. She's picked and continues to pick her men according to two criteria: looks and intellect, which hardly ever coincide in the same person (who knows which box she classified me in?). She once contended with the uber-libertine wife of a big lumber industrialist over a famous Austrian photographer, a very handsome man. Valeria gained the upper hand, and she was still bragging years later. Everybody knew of her numerous short relationships with uninteresting men, nothing more than a few lays: a journalist from the *Nouvel Observateur*, a film cameraman, a TV program planner, but she didn't like to talk about them. Valeria didn't deny these on-the-fly relationships, and she justified herself by saying that in many cases she made love out of "loneliness." Besides "the condo woman," they also called her "the solitary bird" in memory of Leopardi as well as a common sexual metaphor.[2]

What about Clarissa?

I can understand why Zandel wanted to see Clarissa completely naked in public, even though he might have already fucked her that very day in that deplorable village in Corsica. Obviously I will never talk to Clarissa about it. First of all because I already know it would be useless, she would always deny it, even if I were to catch her in bed with Zandel. Denying it to the betrayed husband is a part of many women's ideology. And after all, I fully agree: always deny, up to the end of words.

In an act of imaginary retaliation, I have Valeria get undressed, or rather I slowly undress her with my hands, button by button, the small bra hook, the watchband. She lets me do as I will, as if this were an inevitable rite. Then I, too, get undressed, and we walk around the house, both naked like Zandel and Clarissa in the nudist village. Up yours! Obviously this performance lasts a very short time because after a few minutes we end up in bed. And here, at last, I attack her. First I bang her in every position, my legs intertwined with her legs and arms, my tongue intertwines with her tongue and then moves as smooth as a snail over Valeria's skin. At every new encounter I make up original figures that I record in my personal Kamasutra, so that I can repeat the ones that provided interesting results. Out of them all, I prefer the drunk pecker that flies about on her tits, rises whirling in the air, then dives into the bush. And deep in the bush a concert begins, like saxophone and drill together. I don't think Zandel with his half lung is up to satisfying Clarissa. Often even I can't do it, and I have plenty of breath. At first sight one wouldn't think it, but Clarissa is a nymphomaniac by temperament, and so she's not easy to satisfy. I'm exaggerating a little bit, obviously, but I like to exaggerate when it comes to certain subjects.

After we made love I convinced Valeria to remain naked, and I did too, as we hung around the house. We drink cold water, we get close to the window, we watch the news, only bad news: the stock exchange collapse, a bus of Europeans in Iraq mistakenly targeted by a smart missile launched from an Apache helicopter. The news is getting worse and worse, kamikazes explode, Apaches fly about and days go by. Maybe Bush is happy with the number of deaths on his chest.

The archbishop of Canterbury asked himself where God was when the cataclysm of the tsunami hit: three hundred thousand dead. During his sermon a village priest in Alto Lazio asked himself where was God when they reelected Bush. Some local newspapers protested that Bush is not the tsunami and that clearly Bush prayed to God and God protected him. In fact we already knew, Clarissa said, that God is a bit of a reactionary.

We were still naked like the people visiting that damned nudist village in Corsica. I want to see, I say to myself, if at a certain point it feels normal to walk around the house totally naked and in my imagination to walk around naked even in the street. Unfortunately, sharing this nudity with Valeria doesn't compensate for the encounters that no doubt took place between Clarissa and Zandel. These remain imprinted in my mind and on my eyes. I see them both during the day and at night in bed when I close my eyes to fall asleep. I'm not jealous. I'm only oppressed by too much imagination.

Before I fall asleep the images of those two pass through my mind as if on screen in a movie theater. They are naked, tossing about in bed in the worst, invertebrate positions. I can also hear them moaning, breathing, wheezing deeply and at last the final scream of orgasm. What kind of disgusting story is this? Why can't I get rid of it?

At her place, Valeria is giving me a baffled look, without understanding my sudden distress.

"You are making very strange movements."

"What do you mean?"

"I mean that you're moving your hands and head at random. Strange movements that don't make sense."

"I didn't realize it. It's good of you to tell me."

To tell the truth, when I think it over, I realize I can't control all of my movements. But to put an end to my embarrassment and make our nakedness meaningful, I lay down in bed on top of her, and I once again work my way into her dense bush. In the end I slide inside, accompanied by her moan of pleasure. But I will have to stop trying to give meaning to every move, every gesture and every fuck.

I tested out a sort of problem–riddle on Valeria for the sake of filling one of the many voids in our conversations. A man in the dark has to pick two socks of the same color out of a drawer where the socks are all either red or blue. The question is: how many socks does the man have to grab from the drawer in the dark to have a pair that are certainly of the same color? Valeria answered immediately: three socks. That way, there will be two red and one blue, or two blue and one red or all three the same color, either red or blue. For my part, I smiled out of sympathy. I was hoping that the little riddle would at least embarrass Valeria for a moment, which indeed was what had happened to Zandel when I subjected him to the same stupid question. As a result, I decided to delete the blue-and-red-sock quiz from my repertoire. Moreover, I had noticed that Zandel was upset and almost offended that he hadn't been able to solve such a dumb riddle right away — he who was an expert on the numerical sequences and geometrical calculus of ancient Egypt. One thinks that the riddle is hiding who-knows-what sort of trick behind it, and so one sits there thinking it over, while in fact there is nothing behind it at all. It's a sort of placebo riddle. I have to add that when a university colleague first subjected me to the test, I dodged the question by saying that I would grab only two socks from the drawer, trusting my luck and the calculations of probability. If worse came to worst, who would keep me from going out with one red sock and one blue? These two colors match very well.

The problem of the red and blue socks was absolutely silly, just like the question whether a pound of feathers weighs more than a pound of lead. No, I needed to find something better than the socks in the dark or the pound of lead in order to communicate with my occasional interlocutors and to dispel my attacks of shyness and my political and environmental allergies.

In the meantime the planet Earth, which we all know doesn't care about my problems and my concerns, spins very fast in space with never a moment of rest, while I am tired, and outside it's raining cats and dogs.

Giano seems to be absent-minded, however sometimes he has very subtle perceptions. Mainly he's got suspicious antennas. But most of the time his theoretical ambitions drag him into obscure contradictions. He claims that every gesture causes a series of chain reactions that are destined to create ongoing confrontations, sometimes of a positive nature, but nearly always at the end of the road they produce a catastrophe. As a final sign of negativity, he recounts how, when Ezra Pound was living in Venice, every morning as soon as he got up he opened the window and shouted in a loud voice: "Disaster!" In light of the urban situation in Rome during the postwar boom in building speculation, Giano said that he, too, should repeat the American poet's cry of catastrophe every morning. And he should evaluate the extent to which a young woman who is asked to get totally naked could collide with the Order of Discourse.

Now and then his demolition proposals run into some opposition even from among his students, the majority of whom nevertheless tend to side with him. Giano had a big topographical map of Rome hung up on the wall of the classroom where he holds his classes, as it is precisely in Rome that Giano would like to start his revolution of Complete Urban Deconstruction. This was immediately re-baptized by his students as Urban Utopia, U.U.

To begin with Giano had planned the demolition of entire blocks of the Parioli neighborhood, which is divided into many work zones on the big topographical map. With a green highlighter he had marked off the areas to be demolished. The green meant that those areas were to be transformed into tree-lined gardens or else small squares. Each square, located along the path of an already existing or future metro line, was supposed to feature a cinema or a theater, cafés and restaurants, a supermarket and of course a big underground parking lot. Possibly at some point a nightclub, a gym and a pool.

After the Parioli neighborhood, Giano wanted to dedicate himself to cleaning up Vigna Clara, which simply needed to be "thinned out" by getting rid of every other house. After that it would be time to tackle the problem of the big anthills that were Tuscolana, Appia Nuova and Tiburtina. He said in secret that these neighborhoods should be raised to the ground and rebuilt vertically. Following a progression, one high-rise for every anthill, so that they would occupy a tenth of the ground space but house the same number of people, leaving a lot of space all around, a lot of green, a lot of air, a lot of light. It would be easier to realize his plans for the more civilized suburbs, such as the Quartiere Africano or the Colline Aniene, which could be furnished with big public squares by destroying only a few blocks. It was just a question of making a few strategic choices, and even his students were invited to collaborate on these.

I found out about these things from one of Giano's students who comes here on some afternoons to look for documents in our library for his bachelor's degree thesis. Giano is quite tight-lipped with me about his urban projects. I have the impression that he uses up all his words at the university, where the classes he teaches are apparently much admired, so that there are very few left for when he's home. I also understand that he prefers to write following the thread of his novelistic imagination, as opposed to writing in an ordered way, in the mode of urban-planning.

Unfortunately I am denied even his writings, and I have to secretly take the initiative like a thief if I want to read a few pages of his novel. And thus I discover that Giano, excuse me Bubi, walks around naked at Tania's home, that is Valeria's, and he's not ashamed to write it. (Between you and me, when I read the name Bubi, I hear a dog barking in my ear.) It's strange how in his writing Giano becomes so uninhibited when he talks about sex, himself and Valeria.

Off the record, there's one of his students who often comes by our house to consult books in the library. From the way he looks at me I've gotten the impression he has a special interest in my figure. Certain looks that he gives me.

GIANO

The month of October in Rome is often hot and humid. How could I have refused Zandel and Irina's proposal, which Clarissa immediately approved, to spend a weekend in Fregene? Villa dei Pini is considered the preferred spot to lay down in the shade after a few hours on the beach. It's a relaxing environment under a beautiful pine grove with waiters who run from table to table bringing drinks and coffee. There is nothing more restful than watching others work. Clarissa reprimanded me because, she said, a thought like that is unbearably arrogant for a civilized person.

"Perhaps I'm not a civilized person."

"There you go again, giving me another arrogant answer."

Luckily, petty bickering like this doesn't leave a trace.

We went to the Luna Rossa beach resort to swim in the pool, since the seawater could have seriously harmed our health. Crowded pools repulse me because I always have the feeling that there are sick people among the swimmers. But seawater is really too murky and full of germs, aggressive E. coli.

Clarissa took off her lightweight dress and came out of the changing room in her swimsuit. Gorgeous. She corresponded perfectly to the appearance in the nudist village of the young woman described by Zandel. It was like a slap in the face. Seeing her naked every night had become a habit, and so I always look at her without marvel. But seeing her in a new setting, in public, is something completely different: a radiant appearance that attracted the attention of everybody around. That forty-year-old woman was a miracle of nature, walking with Zandel, who was in his swimsuit as well. Clarissa insisted that Irina and I go in the water. But no pool for me. I stayed under the umbrella with Irina, who had uncovered her pair of bony, wooden legs.

"I don't like the water much. I can barely swim, and I don't like to make a fool of myself," Irina said with the attitude of someone who was revealing an interesting secret.

"Crowded pools physically repulse me. It seems to me as if I'm coming skin to skin with those strangers who feel in their element there."

"I don't believe my husband and Clarissa have any problems on that front."

"Clearly they don't."

"We are here. No coming skin to skin." Irina gave me a contrived smile and added: "Sometimes mixing skin can even happen dry, without dipping into the water."

I didn't know how to respond to such a disarming statement. In the meantime, a strong smell of burning was thickening in the air, as if there were a fire nearby.

"Can you smell that burning?"

"Of course. But who's going to drag us out of here?"

I couldn't understand what she meant, but from her melancholic expression I understood that Irina was asking me for some sort of complicity. This made me sad because there was no way I could meet her expectations.

Is it possible, I said to myself, that among us, men and women, friends and friends' wives, we always have to hint at or engage in sex as the only way out from our daily routine? Don't you realize that even sex becomes routine? Ongoing allusions. On the other hand, a word that rarely occurs in our discussions is love. If that word rarely occurs it means that this feeling rarely occurs, this feeling that is exciting but also demanding and even risky. Only one such case had happened, but it was the makeshift couple of Zandel and the young woman from the pool — God forbid if it were Clarissa. And I don't even know to what extent that story is credible, being so embellished by Zandel.

After Clarissa's and Zandel's swim, we walked to the Villa dei Pini. In the meantime the smell of burning was getting stronger and stronger accompanied by a few light whiffs of smoke entering our nostrils. A passerby informed us that they were burning the dunes in south Fregene, but nothing to worry about. The only inconvenience for those who had houses in the south were the numerous snakes that were fleeing the flames and getting closer to town.

Come, come with your poison. After all, we had decided to safely seek refuge in the shady pine grove of the Villa dei Pini, shady but not quiet because of the deafening chirping of a hundred thousand cicadas. But then, while we were ordering some drinks, Irina suddenly got up and pointed out two snakes on the ground that were approaching our table. We all got up silently, and we moved toward the exit at a fast pace.

Two boys on bikes informed us that hundreds of thousands of snakes had invaded all of Fregene and were hiding inside hedges and in the gardens of the villas. There was probably an element of truth in the two boys' catastrophic embellishments.

"Let's get away from this damned place," said Irina on the verge of a nervous breakdown.

"Let's not exaggerate," said Zandel. But as we turned our eyes, we discovered a small snake next to his BMW, which was parked in the shade of a small back road.

Everything had gone so awry, except perhaps for the pool for Clarissa and Zandel. So we decided to eat something in the first café on the road, a sandwich, a beer, and then we rushed to Rome when the smoke was already close, and the fire trucks' sirens were starting to fill in the air.

Whenever I waste time in such a meaningless way like this weekend in Fregene, I wonder how many pages of my book I could have written if I had stayed in Rome. But instead, I'm there talking about snakes, not a very productive subject for my writing.

I thought he was in his office but instead, through the half-closed bathroom door, I caught Giano in front of the mirror. What was he doing in there? I moved on tiptoe so that I could see him without being seen. Once again, it wasn't my intention to spy on him, but the situation was almost forcing me. Giano was moving slightly closer to the mirror and then pulling himself back, and then he'd move closer again, keeping his gaze fixed in front of him, toward the mirror, with a shadow of mystery on his face. This time at a certain point, I finally understood, or rather I thought I did. Giano was "looking himself in the eye." Was this a challenge? An exorcism? In the end I didn't know how to interpret his strange behavior, just like the last time when his desperate crying or convulsive laughter made me uncomfortable.

"Between you and me" was Giano's usual expression that referred to crucial moments in life, to situations that were extreme or just difficult. A while ago I had decided not to worry too much about his weirdness, and I preferred to ignore those cliffs of negativity that he himself would build, so that he could throw himself off head first. For example, his urban project of destroying entire city blocks to bring air into those Roman neighborhoods stifled by the excessive density of their buildings — I call them buildings but he simply calls them prefabs, without considering the humans who find refuge inside those walls. Beside the need to make the roads less narrow, Giano's project aimed at creating "air bubbles," as he said, which meant making the city more airy, allowing it to breathe. But forget it. It was immediately obvious that Giano was possessed by a destructive genius — malicious people called it urban terrorism — which would have manifested itself regardless of his profession.

This morning I went out, and at the corner of Via Santa Maria dell'Anima and Via dei Coronari, I ran into Adele P., a smart and discreet woman who owns a small building in Via di Panico. Little by little I revealed to her that my husband is developing an urban-planning program for Rome based on the demolition of almost ten per cent of those neighborhoods built since 1940.

"I've heard talk about this project. People discuss it widely, even beyond the university."

"As if it's a bunch of craziness, right?"

"I think it's a fantastic idea, cleaning up Rome's many building horrors. I wish. Even the opinions floating around are anything but negative."

"In any case, we are talking about something weird. If we want to be generous, a utopia."

"Lucky you," she exclaimed. "Can you imagine? Since we've gotten married, my husband has never said anything weird, not one time in his entire life. He's a smart man of great common sense and as densely boring as granite. Better someone a little odd like your husband. After all, I say that urban planning is either creative or it doesn't exist. How I envy you."

I didn't comment on it, but the idea of a husband who was a little crazy clouded my thinking. Was I supposed to complain about Giano's weirdness, his betrayals, the continual hypocrisy that was also our salvation?

My friend suddenly changed the topic.

"Did you hear that Federico Zandel is sick?"

I was shocked, and I didn't know what to say, also because it was strange that she was talking to me about Zandel, as if she were aware of our relationship. But she knew that my husband is an urban planner, I thought, therefore it was logical that she would talk about Zandel, who is also an urban planner.

"I don't know anything," I said, "or rather, I know he had a lung problem a few years back, but he's fine otherwise."

"Oh no, it must be something else. A colleague of his at the university told me about it with an air of mystery. You know who? Precisely your husband, whom I ran into on the street a few days ago."

I didn't want to investigate further, so as not to fuel the gossip — but why doesn't Giano tell me when he meets my girlfriends? I knew about Zandel's poor health — general knowledge, kept quiet in our conversations but confirmed by a few more pages that I had deciphered with difficulty. In Giano's book, or rather in those pages I read here and there, despite my decision to never touch this notebook again, there is some hint at Zurlo's excessive absences from the University. But above all there is a hatred that shines through every line, a strange hatred that starts with the character's name, Zurlo, but which also includes a certain irony about urban planning for sidewalks. In short, in his novel Giano hates Zandel by means of Zurlo, the character who represents him, imitating Zandel's character to a T and later deforming it with all possible malice. While in reality he spends time with Zandel like a dear friend, in his book he describes him with a traitor's sideways glance and pallor. He tries to attribute the evident symptoms of Zandel's weak health to the personal ambiguities of his body. After reading those pages I felt so sick that I took two Laroxyl.

I saw Zandel in the little room next to his office as usual. I didn't ask him about his health, but he seemed calm and loving, in tune with that extraordinary declaration of love pronounced in Giano's presence. We never went back to the topic, but there was a new complicity between us, almost silent: few words, a lot of snuggling, like two small mammals who care for each other. I never felt so happy and sad at the same time as that afternoon in bed together with Zandel.

Forgive me Giano, but I know you already have.

Luigi Malerba

GIANO

I found out from some students that Zandel taught no more than three classes last month. Students are complaining. But I wonder: what does Zandel do with all the time he steals from the university? I know he has business in Holland and negotiations in Zurich, but business trips to those cities, which are just a short plane ride away, don't justify so much absence.

Someone says that Zandel is sick, but I wouldn't know whom to ask for any news. Certainly not him because of an obvious discretion and because we always try to avoid discussion of our personal physiology. I could ask Clarissa, who might know something, but it's a very remote possibility because at home I avoid talking about Zandel just as Clarissa never talks about Valeria. At this point our second relationships are integrated and recorded in silence, but this time it's different because we have a perfect excuse to talk: Zandel's absences from the university are a valid question mark.

"What do I know about it? He must have his reasons," Clarissa says distractedly. I immediately understood that she wants to avoid the subject. In fact she shrugs her shoulders and goes into the kitchen. Exaggerated. And I thought she would enjoy that I was offering her the chance to talk about her lover.

Yesterday, my project to "thin out" some Roman neighborhoods stirred up criticism once again, but in the majority of cases I obtain clear signs of enthusiasm from my students. Obviously my projects bother a lot of people. For example, tearing to pieces some blocks next to Via Archimede, a winding and seemingly luxurious alley that is constantly backed up, which starts from Piazza Euclide, proceeds uphill for a long stretch towards Piazza Pitagora, then repents and goes back the same length, veering down towards Maresciallo Pilsudski Boulevard. It's one of the most absurd streets in the whole of Parioli. You can't go down it without cursing, and often it gives drivers the Labyrinth Effect, with dizziness and gagging.

Was it worth wasting Archimedes's name on this street, which is the sublime portrait of stupidity in urban planning? And what about, lower down, Euclid's name on a chaotic square, a carousel full of cars that go uphill towards Parioli or downhill towards dry Acqua Acetosa? Even Pythagoras was caught up in the urban-planning horror of this part of Parioli. No bulldozers for my Urban Deconstruction, but dynamite. I agree: sometimes I exaggerate.

Let's be honest, we're shocked by the mistakes made in Rome after the Forties, but we also forget about the mistakes that were made during the golden age of Roman architecture. Just to recall one of them, go take a look at the sumptuous sixteenth and seventeenth-century buildings in the historic center: majestic facades that are impossible to encompass in your gaze because a building that is just as sumptuous was built directly opposite, at a minimal distance across the street. And these streets are too narrow even for coaches, in particular in the Torre Argentina neighborhoods and the surrounding area. But the errors of the ancients don't justify those of the moderns, which we could make up for by eliminating not the sumptuous Renaissance and Baroque buildings, but architectural terrors that nobody would ever miss.

Fine, my colleagues and some of my students say, luckily it's only a utopia because it implies the destruction of many blocks, which would cause the violent opposition of the owners and, in the hypothetical case of a decision in favor of eminent domain, it would cost the State astronomical sums. And where would the owners of the destroyed properties end up living? A student of mine, who lives right in Via Archimede and saw the block including his house covered in green marker, asked me where his eventual destination would be.

"Will I perhaps have to end up in Centocelle?" he asked. "Or in Spinaceto?"

These are all objections that I foresaw and that don't call into question the civic value of my project. However, they do postpone its realization to more evolved times, times even richer than our own.

Some architecture colleagues understood that, were even the smallest part of my project ever to be accepted — for instance, in the areas constructed according to the logic of building speculation like the Quadraro or the Quartiere Africano — it would create jobs for the redevelopment of new spaces after the demolition: skyscrapers and gardens. All considered, a great deal of work for architects, who in principle agree that it's time to demolish.

At home I don't like to talk about my theories, which are all projected towards the future and are the preferred subject of my classes. But I'm sure Clarissa is perfectly up to date on everything thanks to the interrogations she inflicts on the students who visit my library. And I think this must be sufficient because, perhaps also due to my handwriting, she doesn't seem interested in reading the notebook entitled U.D., which stands for Urban

Deconstruction, that I left on my desk like *The Purloined Letter* by Edgar Allan Poe. She doesn't even read the articles that I publish now and then in *Diagonale*, the journal of the Department of Architecture of Valle Giulia.

CLARISSA

During a hunting expedition in the Langhe, King Vittorio Emanuele II encounters a peasant who removes his hat as a sign of respect. The king pulls a cigar out of his pocket and offers it to the peasant, who utters: "Majesty, this cigar is the most beautiful day of my life!"

Giano tells this little story at a restaurant with some colleagues, urban planners and architects, Zandel included. But he immediately feels the need to say that he detests both hunting and Savoys of any rank or generation.

"The identification of the cigar with the most beautiful day of the peasant's life looks to be a rhetorical figure," says Giano. "But which one?"

Nobody knows how to answer, and so, with a childish smile, Giano admits his uncertainty. But he adds that perhaps it's an anomalous form of metonymy.

"In that case, would the cigar be at once the cause and the effect of the peasant's happy day?" I ask timidly.

"Precisely, a paradoxical metonymy, which identifies the cause with the effect."

The strange thing is that, while Giano was recounting his little story, in my ears I heard a crash of metal sheets and the desperate voice of the victim from the fatal accident on the road between Frankfurt and Duisburg where our friend, the German journalist, had perished. Was this a mistake or my subconscious' distraction? Could it be that I have such a defective subconscious? I didn't know how to find the cause of my bothersome, grim slip. Oh please, what does the likable Johannes Westerhoff have to do with Vittorio Emanuele II?

Giano is pathetically naive, and I've tried in vain to make him understand that it would be better if he refrained from such exhibitions. Even though everybody liked the little story, not everybody liked the little rhetoric lesson, in which I intervened so as not to let it fall into the void.

Giano is the least sociable person in the world, and he knows it. With these little narrative exhibitions he participates to some degree in the frivolous events we sometimes take part in. Mostly, art openings or book presentations on architecture and urban planning. These nearly always end up at a restaurant where Giano performs, actually earning a certain amount of attention, though I'm not sure how sincere. But he knows what he's doing, since these little stories of his allow him to avoid, free of charge, the convivial polemics on his urban planning. If, later, a political discussion is brought up, he then begins to blow his nose and sneeze thanks to his sudden allergic Leftist reactions.

Based on my extremely tiring reading of a few more pages of his novel, it would appear that Giano understood not only that I too went to the nudist village, but also that the beautiful young woman Zandel described in the pool was me, Clarissa in the flesh, all forty years of her. Is it a fictional invention? The sexual activity in the bungalow was frenetic, a narrative obsession. I hope Giano simply happened on a situation that was useful for his plot and took advantage of it without realizing it corresponded to that impulsive business that we stubbornly call reality.

But how dare Giano, my husband, put me in the pages of his book in such a shameless way? That the events end up corresponding to the truth is no justification. On the contrary. Who authorizes him to ascribe to me feelings, and worse, sexual activities he can't prove? It's too easy to write a novel this way, pilfering ideas, facts and characters from family and friends. I hope Giano has no intention of publishing this phalanstery of bizarre erotic displays since readers could easily recognize its real protagonists.

I dropped an unbreakable glass on the kitchen floor, and it exploded and crumbled into a thousand tiny fragments. They explained to me that unbreakable glasses have a vulnerable point, a sort of Achilles' heel that, if hit, causes the glass to explode and shatter.

Careful Giano, if you hit me in my Achilles' heel, I too can explode like an unbreakable glass, or a kamikaze.

I'm joking, of course. Sometimes I like to joke.

GIANO

Clarissa and I are not unrestrained enough to confess our sins to each other. We prefer silence, a formidable adhesive for situations that otherwise would end up shattering into pieces, like the unbreakable glass that fell from Clarissa's hands onto the kitchen floor this morning. Only as an adult did I learn that there is a very subtle reality beyond myself, and it has to be respected with a great deal of discretion, sometimes even with secrecy and a great deal of silence.

Clarissa makes strange demands. Now she's got it into her head that I need to take her to Strasbourg, to the small hotel in front of the cathedral. I believe I understand the reason for this strange demand: Clarissa probably found out about my meeting with Valeria in Strasbourg, and she wants to repeat the same trip as well. This would demonstrate to me but also to herself that she is just as good as Valeria and deserves the same attention. I insist that she explain the reason for her request, knowing full well that she will never tell me the truth, too viscous for either of us.

"What does it matter?" answers Clarissa.

"A shred of an explanation," I insist, knowing that I am walking on the edge of a cliff.

"There's not always a clear and comprehensible explanation."

"I'm not interested in an obscure and incomprehensible explanation, and since I don't want to force you to justify your request, I surrender. All right, next Saturday I'm taking you to Strasbourg."

"To the small hotel in front of the cathedral."

"I agree, to the small hotel in front of the cathedral. I'll make a reservation."

When she hears that I'm willing to go back to Strasbourg with her, Clarissa calms down and keeps quiet.

I wonder who told her about my meeting with Valeria. Morpurgo the architect is the only one who could have known the particulars of the small hotel in front of the cathedral. He could have learned about it from the concerned party during their night in the sleeper car. But how did the news get from Morpurgo to Clarissa? There are thousands of eyes and thousands of ears. Obviously I can't ask her, but once again I satisfy myself with noting for the thousandth time that words fly from one person to another like cold germs.

With this absurd demand Clarissa gave me another topic for my book. Thank you, thank you for your collaboration.

Zandel told me that Giano has discovered the existence of a large obelisk that has remained buried for who-knows-how-long in the area where the sixteenth-century Palazzo Madama was built, now the seat of the Senate. It was rediscovered right in front of the palazzo, during some excavations to repair a gas line in Corso Rinascimento. The tip of the obelisk made it all the way to the street, and the rest was stretched out below Palazzo Madama. The workers immediately covered it back up with dirt on the orders of Romana Gas so as to avoid the procession of archeologists and curious onlookers. But the news had already leaked out, and the obelisk underneath the Senate had become a topic of discussion in the Roman newspapers.

Another obelisk is located under Palazzo Santacroce in Piazza Cairoli. It was discovered during some work in the cellars and kept secret. It seems that Giano taught a class about these two obelisks, real treasurers buried in the subsoil of Rome, just like gold and diamonds are hidden in mines. Everybody knows that Rome is an infinite mine of precious buried antiques.

Giano presented these two pieces of news with the few details he knew, and then he questioned his students, hoping that someone would suggest destroying Palazzo Madama and Palazzo Santacroce, at least partially, in order to dig up the obelisks. Especially Palazzo Madama, frequented by those awful senators. No student dared propose the destruction of those two buildings, despite the fact that they knew about their professor's penchant for demolition. Giano was disappointed and remained lost in thought during the rest of the class, grumbling indecipherable things, as if waiting for a word from the audience. The students were severely embarrassed with some murmurs of amazement or perhaps disagreement.

It's humiliating that I'm only able to get this news about my husband by way of my lover. But after all, I prefer that Giano doesn't talk to me about his urban-planning projects because I already know he would not accept my take on them and even less so a possible critique. As a result, there would be a reason for an argument, and we prefer to live in harmony. Nor do I insist that he tell me anything about the novel he's writing, as you would normally expect. The two initials on the cover are his unhappy attempt to mislead yours truly. After all, Clarissa doesn't notice anything, according to him.

We can allow ourselves a few, petty disagreements, for example about the little stories he tells that always embarrass me or his obsession with the poisons in food and the air. But Zandel explained to me that it's not just about food or environmental ecology, but political ecology. Environmental poisons — and Zandel agrees with Giano — are symmetrical and complementary to a particular allergy against four genetically modified political types. As soon as they appear on TV, the remote springs into action to change the channel. Even in his sleep, Giano continually repeats what a great invention the remote is.

"Giano is an allergically committed man," says Zandel, and this is one of the few ironic statements that he allows himself to make about Giano for a while. He talks about Giano as little as possible, but the few times he does he speaks with consideration and only rarely with lighthearted irony. I asked him whether he has any news about the book Giano is writing. He doesn't know anything about it.

"That's weird," Zandel says, "because Giano always tells me about his projects. He even keeps me updated on the articles he's writing or thinking about writing." Naturally I didn't reveal to him that it's a novel, but instead I told him about the initials on the notebook's cover.

"A solemn weirdness," says Zandel. "Are you sure about those initials?"

"Positive."

"They could be the initials for Urban Deconstruction, but also the name of a secret mistress of his."

"No, because his secret mistress's name is Valeria. She's so secret that everyone knows."

"You're kidding."

"I thought you knew about it, too."

"I prefer not to know."

I understood that even Zandel plays at hypocrisy. So, I'm surrounded by hypocrisy all around. I, too, belong to this circle. More comedy than tragedy in any case.

God willing, I will never write a novel — although if Giano writes one I could as well, why not? And now, don't go thinking that I'm mad at Giano because he's writing a novel. Please.

Giano

"First ethics, then science." A stranger's hand wrote this maxim in red spray paint on the outside wall of the building I live in. Is it perhaps directed at me? My neighbors in the building are very nice, good morning and good evening, but no doubt they have very little interest in either ethics or science. A luxury upholsterer on the first floor, an executive for the San Paolo Bank of Turin and a bachelor photographer on the second floor, and Clarissa and I are on the third floor.

Whomever it is directed at — perhaps just to passersby — I can't manage to understand what the unknown street philosopher wants to convey to his occasional readers by proposing this elementary priority of ethics over science. Certainly it's a maxim and project of vast perspectives, which, if they were applied, could have changed many things in the world. Just for starters in 1945, Truman wouldn't have launched the two atomic bombs on Hiroshima and Nagasaki, three hundred thousand dead. First ethics, then the Bomb. No, dear Truman, the *before* and *after* don't work this way. Later he died, too. Truman, just like the inhabitants of those two Japanese cities. And I don't wish it on him to run into them in the Beyond, all those Japanese who died in Hiroshima and Nagasaki.

Assuming that what was written was directed at me, what remains to be understood is whether it's an assertion, a plea, an invitation or a challenge. Should I perhaps feel guilty for betraying ethics since I'm an adulterer? But Clarissa is the only person in the world who can reprimand me, not the unknown street philosopher. And instead, she doesn't even dream of blaming me since she, too, is just as guilty from an ethical point of view. The fact that ethics comes before science matters very little to me, since I have only an occasional and superficial relationship with science, unless you consider urban planning a science. However, the creative and paradoxical urban planning that I'm involved with is certainly excluded from the field of science.

Clarissa knows perfectly well that ethics is not a goal for her or for me. She nonchalantly pretended not to notice the statement, although it's written on the wall of our building with red paint and in capital letters.

Since I told her all right, next week I'll take you to Strasbourg, and we'll go by plane, even though I would have preferred if you had come with me for those three days during the conference like

I had proposed, Clarissa hasn't said another word about Strasbourg or the small hotel in front of Notre-Dame Cathedral. It's clear that she wanted to inflict a purely virtual punishment on me.

This call to ethics evoked an incident from a secret nest in my memory. That incident had increased the sincere but fragmentary admiration I've always had for Clarissa. Her parents had a house in the area surrounding Genzano, where Clarissa and I often used to go to spend our weekends, a month in the summer and ten days at Christmas every year. We had become friends with their old female German Sheperd, who got excited every time we arrived. Over the past few times, we had found her to be very depressed, and she walked shuffling her rear legs. Clarissa's parents had told us that she was very old and sick, but they didn't feel like putting her down as the veterinarian had suggested. One Saturday we found the dog, who had gone to die in front of the entrance to the house. She wasn't moving, she would no longer get up, and sometimes she would shake and wheeze.

"She's dying, poor thing," Clarissa's parents had said.

We remained silent, looking at the poor dog who had come to die right in front of her masters' eyes. Clarissa and I remained silent before the painful spectacle of the agony of that poor animal we had such affection for. Pain and much embarrassment on my part, as I couldn't wait to escape from the devastating spectacle. But suddenly Clarissa got close to the dog and bent down to pet her on the head. It was a gesture of great sympathy before death. The dog moved just barely in an attempt to lift her head as if she wanted to thank her.

I will always remember that compassionate and very humane gesture, and it is one of the reasons why I admire and love Clarissa. Who knows if this, too, is the ethics mentioned on the wall of our building.

CLARISSA

I am sure Giano understood why I wanted to go to Strasbourg with him and why I wanted to stay in the small hotel in front of Notre-Dame Cathedral. Of course he understood. Giano and I have been sending indirect messages to each other for a while now, sometimes solemn gibes like this one over Strasbourg.

Now it happens that a few other pages of Giano's novel have upset me deeply. I don't understand how he managed to guess so many of my secrets. As if he were spying on me through the keyhole, as if he could read my thoughts each night in the hours of perfect solitude when I lie still in bed, waiting to fall asleep.

Between you and me, I've never suffered from insomnia, but the past few nights I've lain in bed with my thoughts, my eyes closed for two or three hours before I fall asleep. This can almost be called insomnia. I was afraid of entering the downward spiral of sleeping pills. They are like a drug because it seems that later on it's hard to come off them. But I couldn't even understand the reasons for my insomnia. One fine day I read in a magazine insert for women that in certain African tribes, whoever suffers from insomnia lies there yawning, one yawn after the other, until falling asleep. Despite the dubious journalistic source, I tried the experiment and used my yawning as a sleeping pill: the effect as a treatment of the cause. It worked. After about a quarter hour of yawning in hypnotic repetition, I slowly entered the silent corridor of sleep.

Giano was a little surprised by all my yawning, but when I explained to him that I was using it as a sleeping pill, he seemed interested and satisfied. Actually Giano is always more prepared to understand the paradoxical sides of life than the rational ones, although every other day he claims that he is analogic and Cartesian. These are claims that confirm his paradoxical self-consciousness. Why analogic? Why Cartesian? I didn't ask any questions, so as not to embarrass him and especially because you cannot expect a reason for everything, least of all for a few innocent adjectives.

Obviously, I never told him that the pages of his book were the reason for my insomnia. Never, ever. They were skewering my thoughts and feelings and my secret desires.

GIANO

I've realized that Clarissa got her hands on my notebook. As a result, she probably found out that I'm writing a novel and not a treatise on Urban Deconstruction, as those two initials on the cover were supposed to make her believe. In any case, I don't know how far she'll be able to read my writing. But she will be petrified if my novel is published one day, because I can't help but involve her and that pig, Zandel, in the story. My imagination runs like crazy, following the thread of betrayals, and in the end I'm almost sure it's nearing the truth.

In the meantime the condominium association in Governo Vecchio decided to repaint the façade of our building, full of dusty stains and crusts. The administrator came to urge a decision on the color. We chose a pale color, between yellow and green, which had previously been proposed during a prior meeting of the condominium residents.

"So the light-shit color, then" the administrator said during the meeting. He was an arrogant and sardonic man. Everyone was shocked.

"We all agree on the light-shit color," I underlined, to deflate his attempt at intimidating us.

The work will start in three to four months. Thus at a certain point, the statement, "First ethics, then science," will disappear. These words cause a sort of mental whirlpool that accompanies me every time I go out or come back through the building entry. I don't know whether the thing displeases me or not.

I don't always manage to pinpoint with clarity my opinions on ideas, things, people and graffiti.

With a struggle I managed to read a few more pages of Giano's notebook with those initials on the cover that still offend me. Well then, the fact that his novel is inspired by people and events from Giano's own experience doesn't strike me as a great idea for a writer. Big deal, we are the main characters, Giano and I, then Zandel and I. In the few pages I've read, it doesn't seem that Irina, Zandel's wife, is present, and I think that bitch, Valeria, is barely mentioned. In any case I admit that I'm very curious to see what life has in store for me according to Giano's imagination in the pages I haven't managed to read yet.

But what a strange feeling of dizziness, finding myself described in a novel. I am Marozia, it's clear, but what confuses my soul is finding my thoughts and my behavior written down. I must say, they are often more reasoned and plausible than my real thoughts and behavior, which are always so uncertain and disconnected. Giano makes me move and talk like a puppet under his command. And the feeling that Marozia is behaving in a more reasonable and, let's say it, more intelligent way than I behave does nothing but create a little more confusion. It makes me understand that it's possible to lead around a paper character however one wants, to make it do whatever pleases the writer and is convenient for the plot. In contrast, in reality I follow instincts and feelings that to me are often random and therefore unpredictable. Giano's bet is to steal my life and translate it, for better or for worse, into a paper Marozia, and he does so according to his mood and the supposed needs of the novel. It's too easy and too romantic to write that Marozia is such a magnetic beauty that it makes Zurlo (Zandel) fall instantly in love. But this time not only does reality look like what Giano wrote, it's even more romantic and novel-like — even if I'm not able to forget that I'm forty-two years old and not twenty. Luckily for me, whoever sees my forty-year-old knees does me a favor by going around to tell people about them. And I can also lay my hands and my tits on the table.

So, his crazy Urban Deconstruction is not enough for Giano, now he also has ambitions to write a novel. I think it's like inventing a city that is already all wrapped up, with its inhabitants houses streets squares buildings monuments the train station the gardens the hospital underpasses the little fountains the sidewalks the markets the one-way streets. Wait a second, Giano is having fun here moving his pawns around, the men and women stolen

from life following a complete hypothesis of fictional reality —
otherwise I would have to think that Giano knows all the secrets
of our relationship, I mean between me and Zandel. To the point
that sometimes I feel like I'm doing things I've already read about
in Giano's pages. He seems to retrace people, places, behavior
and the real vices of the two of us and of our friends. And often
he even anticipates them to embroider them over his story. I'm
sure he's writing a bad novel, certainly a false one like those that
pretend to describe so-called reality. Luckily there's no trace of
Heidegger, despite the pervasive rapture that Zandel pointed out
with perverse irony.

I'm very curious to go on reading it, but now I close the
notebook back up and put it away with care. I do this so that
Giano won't notice I've been handling it, but above all because,
in the struggle to decipher his impossible handwriting, I've got
an atrocious headache. To be honest, I can't blame my headache
exclusively on his bad handwriting.

GIANO

I am almost a little sorry that after her threat, Clarissa gave up on taking a new trip to Strasbourg with me. Or at least this is what I think I can gather, since she stopped talking about it. Getting there by plane, one night at the small hotel in front of the cathedral and then returning in the sleeper car the following night. The hotel is discreet and pleasant, in part because of how quiet the pedestrian area around the cathedral is, where even taxis are not allowed to drive. I would have taken Clarissa through the flower market. I would have given her a bunch of cyclamens just like I gave to Valeria. Then we would have gone together to get a good latte with a croissant while sitting outside at a café in Rue des Juifs behind the cathedral — the same café where Valeria and I sat. I would have studied the waiter's face to see if he recognized me: back here again after two weeks but with a different woman, one very different from the first. I would have been curious to notice if the flower woman also recognized me. Two weeks later, she would have sold me the same bunch of cyclamens for a different woman from the first one.

I was already thinking about duplicating the gestures and the paths I took with Valeria as a secret revenge, a wickedness Clarissa wouldn't have suspected. To satisfy herself she would have simply been content to have me repeat the same trip to Strasbourg, but I would have made her revenge backfire on her without her knowing it.

I am ruminating over useless thoughts because once she had my agreement Clarissa stopped talking about the trip to Strasbourg, and it certainly won't be me who'll remind her.

LUIGI MALERBA

And if one fine day we decided to tell each other everything, to confess our by now institutionalized betrayals, while sitting comfortably in our living room with lit cigarettes, both of us even though I don't smoke? At this point it's clear that my relationship with Zandel and the one between Giano and Valeria are no longer secret except for appearances. Giano pretends to be busy at the university when he goes to Valeria's, and I simply go out to run small errands without accounting for it to Giano. It's easy for me to spend an afternoon here and there with Zandel. It would even be a monotonous routine if my desire and love weren't sustaining me: a love heated up by Zandel's crazy declaration.

Giano spied on me for a long time to confirm his suspicions, but as soon as he felt sure of my betrayals, he stopped spying on me. Giano knows that I couldn't live without him even if I hated him. It's a warm and silent hate that reinforces my love. It's not a contradiction, and even if it were?

Unfortunately Zandel has suddenly left for New York, where he's meeting with a commission on the reconstruction of Iraq — for the moment they'll go on destroying it. It's a non-demanding meeting, just to record the opinion of an Italian urban planner, so he told me. Later on they will decide whether Italy will take part in the Great Banquet of Reconstruction, which has already been bought up for the most part by American companies — some of them had signed contracts for the reconstruction even before the destruction, right after the beginning of the war.

Before he left, Zandel told me he knows less than nothing about Iraq, but this was going to be an absolutely informal meeting, suggested by a Canadian member of the commission, whom Zandel had met while touring Morocco. Together they had seen the Roman architecture — the remains of Roman architecture — in Volubilis, but most of all, the remains of the Arabic architecture in Fes and Meknes. They had debated their different opinions on the two cultures and architectures: the Canadian urban planner was all for Roman architecture, Zandel was all for the Arabic. A solid and transparent friendship was born of that discussion and their opposing opinions, and now the Canadian urban planner had asked Zandel to express his opinion at the UN Commission of Inquiry.

A week later Zandel called me on my cellphone to say that his stay in New York would be prolonged another ten or so days: bad bronchitis and a touch of fever due to the lethal air conditioning of the skyscrapers — every time it was a jump to the North Pole from ninety degrees on the street. This was announced in a sad and far away voice, broken by stormy gusts of wind from the Atlantic crossing. Zandel always said that one has to leave Rome in order to see the rainbow. Had he seen the rainbow in New York? No, he replied, he couldn't see it without me. I welcomed this news as a sign of our shared destiny.

After that phone call, no news for a week, and then for fifteen days. I thought about everything, even an American affair, recalling Zandel's many mistresses, which Giano had told me about. I thought about Zandel discovering a serious illness that he wanted to hide from me or some stupid accident he was embarrassed to admit.

Giano and Zandel's colleagues immediately thought the worst when his wife went to be with him in New York. And in Rome there was nobody else who could give us any news. I couldn't express my worry, and the silence I had imposed on myself in those circumstances made his absence even more painful for me. One day I caught myself silently crying while I stopped to look at shop windows in the streets around the Pantheon. A window reflected my image, including two big tears that were falling down my cheeks and mingling with the pearls of a necklace on display behind the security glass. I purchased that necklace so I could wear it when Zandel heals. But I already knew I would never put it on. Maybe never. It's better to leave space open to a light breeze of hope.

Giano locked up the drawer where he keeps his novel, but he left the key in the keyhole. As if he was saying, "Look, I know you're reading my notebook, but if you really insist you have to unlock the drawer with the key."

For the moment Clarissa can resist.

I'm worried about Clarissa. Her lover has been in New York for almost two months, and we haven't heard anything more from him. The university registrar received a telegram from Zandel, which justifies his absence "for serious health issues." It is true that in order to justify such a long absence he needed to write that his health issues were serious. But everything leads one to think that the reasons really are serious, ever since his wife went to be with him in New York.

Clarissa is crestfallen, and I can't even comfort her. I have to pretend to believe that she's just having a sudden fit of exhaustion, which often happens to her when the rainy season arrives. At a certain point I asked her if she knew anything about Zandel, because I know that talking about your sorrows sometimes can be a relief.

"How would I know?" she answered. "I know what you know, that is, nothing."

Clarissa's irritation was not directed at me. She was simply offended by Zandel's prolonged absence and the lack of news. More than being offended or irritated by the lack of news, I, too, was worried. This was because I knew that in New York Zandel and his wife were hiding the truth from us, and I feared that at any moment something irreparable could happen. What, for example? So as not to suffer ahead of time, I tried to erase any thought of Zandel, because every thought was leading me in the direction of his illness and death. Poor Zandel, I could already see him, lying down in his coffin with a wax face and his hands crossed over his chest — a morbid image. I even dreamed about him, together with Clarissa, who was desperately crying as she accompanied him to the Verano.

I was very bothered by these nighttime images, and I sought to exorcize them in every way, with stupid attempts to diminish the gravity of the situation, which was by now evident.

"He's probably over his fixation on the nudist villages, I'd imagine."

Clarissa turned on me, furious.

"My compliments on your fine sensitivity. We have a friend who is sick, perhaps very sick, and you trot out the most vulgar topic to make fun of the poor soul."

Beneath her words was the shadow of sorrow. Clarissa was right, I had committed a gaffe, a vulgar gaffe with regard to a friend. I didn't even try to justify myself because I was sure that Clarissa had also had the gravest thoughts about Zandel's health. How many times did we put him to death in those days? How many times did we lay him down in a coffin and accompany him to the cemetery? We even put down a bouquet of chrysanthemums on his tomb. In those days, I profusely ascribed my funereal imagination to Clarissa as well. In the meantime I was taking back my poisonous fantasies about the African swamp.

Now the rain floods down on the dead and the living, the days go by in Rome just like in New York, and the Stock Exchange continues to go down.

I had a dream. I usually retain a vague memory of my dreams, but this time I remember everything, even a lot of meaningless details. Above all, I remember my calm state of mind and, if you can say this about a dream, a feeling of slight happiness, scattered and a bit blurry around the edges.

I arrived at the elevator of a building that I knew by heart, but I found a sign hanging on the door: "Out of service." It didn't bother me, and I was almost happy that it gave me the chance to climb the stairs. The entrance hall, the elevator and especially the stairs, the grey marble steps, the iron handrail, everything was perfectly familiar to me, even though the image of the person whom I was going to visit hadn't yet appeared in the video of my dream.

When I arrived on the third floor with lightness, step after step as if the force of gravity were cancelled out, I found myself in front of two big doors, which I immediately recognized. The left one had a brass tag, "Arch. Federico Zandel," while on the right one there was only a peephole and the outline of two keyholes. While I was moving my finger toward the doorbell, the right door opened and Zandel appeared as if he had guessed my presence. With a gesture he invited me to come inside, and he walked with me into the tiny kitchen of his private studio, next to the big office. I sat down facing him, in front of a coffee table with a crystal fruit bowl on top, full of fruits of every kind, without regard to the season: apples bananas strawberries grapes kiwi cherries pineapple and a round white fruit that was barely bigger than an apple. I stretched out my hand to take the unknown fruit, but Zandel shook his head no.

"Why not?" I asked.

"You have to be patient, and one day we'll eat it together."

My hand was still reaching for the fruit.

"Please."

"Not now."

"You are not Adam, and I am not Eve. We can eat what we want without sin."

"What do you mean? Don't you realize that this is the Earthly Paradise?"

Zandel stood up, and I did as well, without tasting any of those marvelous fruits. He took me in his arms, and he held me tight for a long while. I felt a heat all over my body, I'd say of happiness and desire. Or at least that's how the emotion of that embrace seems in my memory. I still remember with infinite nostalgia that feeling, truly belonging to the Earthly Paradise, which I never felt with this intensity in reality. Or is it perhaps my memory that amplifies the sensations of that dream?

It was natural that our encounter would end up in bed. Zandel started to unbutton my little blouse, and little by little he completely undressed me with lightness and ease, as one peels a banana. I found myself standing naked, but still in my shoes and stockings. I had an expansive feeling of my beauty. Every gesture was soft and fluffy. There was a great silence all around and, like a breeze, a light music in the distance, just maybe the saxophone of Coleman Hawkins, who always accompanies me in moments of great emotional intensity. All of this looked like the idea of happiness to me. I took off my shoes and stockings and lay down on the bed, while Zandel undressed himself in a flash. He got on top of me, beginning the ritual of preliminary kissing. He caressed me everywhere, and finally he penetrated me while the music was wrapping us up softly and solemnly.

After making love in my dream, I woke up still feeling the memory of that happiness on top of me. Immediately I remembered that Zandel was in New York, and nobody was able to give me — damn it! — any news about his health. At my side, Giano was in a deep sleep.

I thought back to my dream again. Actually, excluding the enchanted atmosphere, in my dream I had repeated one of my encounters with Zandel, which all unfolded in more or less the same way. I haven't seen him for more than two months, and the dream unfolded in an atmosphere of happiness suspended over an abyss, because from one moment to the next I expect bad news from New York.

But I can't understand what the white fruit in the kitchen was, and Adam's promise will remain disappointed because Eve obviously can't hope that he'll keep a promise made in a dream when he's awake. As far as I'm concerned, the white fruit simply doesn't mean anything. You can't expect to give a meaning to everything that appears in a dream, and often not even to things that belong — as Giano would say — to so-called reality.

GIANO

According to the bits of half-news that were wandering along the corridors of the university at Valle Giulia, it seemed that Zandel was basically dying in New York. His return lowered the dramatic tone of those voices. Zandel came back to Rome in good shape, so to speak. He invited us to dinner and serenely explained that he'd had a damned viral pneumonia, one of those you can catch on the plane when the air conditioning circulates some infected person's virus. In New York they wanted to treat it with a series of radiation treatments, a new therapy that, according to them, had already shown great results. Instead, as a result, there was a problem with his red blood cells, with those son-of-a-bitch red blood cells, Zandel said, but nothing dramatic.

The atmosphere at dinner was relaxed, with a few comments about the recipe for the Mapie de Toulouse-Lautrec hazelnut and coffee dessert, which Irina had prepared. Later, she told us, jokingly, that she had gone to meet her husband because she could not leave him alone in New York, where Italian men are snapped up like hot cakes. But why did she feel the need to give an explanation for her trip to New York? Such a mundane and phony explanation.

The final comment of the evening was that now Zandel will have to undergo some treatments here in Italy, a real torture.

Zandel lives in a nice house in Via del Consolato, between Corso Vittorio Emanuele and Via Giulia, so Clarissa and I walked back from there. While walking, we told each other that Zandel's news about his health hadn't convinced us. When has anyone ever treated pneumonia with radiation?

"Never heard of such a thing. That radiation treatments could then create a problem with his red blood cells is easy to understand."

"Blood disorders, red and white cells, it's all worrisome, whatever the reason, yet those two wanted us to believe they are unconcerned. Did you see how pale Zandel is? You can see at a glance that he's missing red blood cells."

Sometimes Clarissa seems like an ass with her extreme simplifications and drowsy thoughts suited to a casual stroll.

"What has that got to do with it? He's always been as pale as a squeezed lemon, even before New York and before his illness."

"I'm just saying that they could open up with their friends."

Clarissa seemed sincerely displeased by the lack of closeness on the part of the two Zandels, husband and wife.

"You're right. Just lies, as if the illness were something shameful."

"That solemn lie about radiation treatments for viral pneumonia is even offensive."

"They are treating us like two illiterates. He's worse than his wife."

"His wife is worse," Clarissa pointed out.

"Not really. His wife tries to get by and follows her husband's lead."

"No, no. She's worse."

"In that case, end of conversation."

I was irritated by Clarissa's inappropriate confidence. Let's put it like this: as I already knew, it's impossible to talk to Clarissa about Zandel. We arrived at our building entrance without saying another word. Here, on the wall of our building, Clarissa read out the statement that had been there for several weeks. Clarissa hates graffiti.

"'First ethics, then science.' What is it supposed to mean?"

"The meaning is clear, and it's quite important. What would matter, instead, is to understand at whom it's directed."

"I think it's simply directed at everyone who passes by here and stops to read this boring and pedantic statement."

"Well, even at the two of us, who pass by here three or four times a day."

"What an honor."

"In a few months they will redo the color of the façade, and they'll cover both ethics and science with paint."

Yesterday afternoon I went to Zandel's, and I found that a sign was hanging on the elevator: "Out of service." Just like in my dream. I didn't attribute any special meaning to what was certainly a simple coincidence. I took the stairs, well aware of the heavy force of gravity on the earth: one hundred and twenty pounds, one step after another.

Zandel welcomed me as usual with a light kiss on my lips, then we sat down on the two little armchairs of his small living room.

"You are finally healed. You know, we feared for your health."

"I'm fine, but I'm not healed. Do you understand the difference?"

"Are you saying you have an illness that can't be seen?"

"Those are the worst."

"Should I be worried?"

"I will tell you in a few days, after my visit to the hematologist. In New York I did a treatment that butchered my red blood cells."

"Such a violent treatment?"

"Do you remember Chernobyl? I will have to stay away from kids and pregnant women, at least for a while. I'm radioactive."

At the word Chernobyl I became frightened, and I didn't ask anymore. Zandel came to sit on the armrest of the big chair and hugged me. Many small kisses, many airy words of love. We didn't plan to make love. I was shocked, but I didn't want him to notice, so the subject shifted to New York.

"Being sick in New York, costs aside, must have compromised your relationship with the city. It's an energetic city. That's the effect it had on me the two times I went there with Giano, each time for two weeks, which is enough to love a city. It's even possible to fall in love with New York at first sight, as soon as you set foot on your first street there and breathe your first breath of Atlantic air."

Certainly because of his illness, Zandel must have had different feelings in New York.

"You called it an energetic city, but it's also a place where one can die with lightness, without the funereal ornamentation of many Italian cities. Not just Venice with its gondolas as black as a bier and the dead water of its small canals. There is even something mortuary about Palermo: the lush botanic garden is a funereal garden — it smells like a cemetery — the old abandoned buildings in Via Maqueda, the outskirts with no glimmer of humanity, the battered, crusty churches."

I was uncomfortable with Zandel's words. He was so serene and lucid, so resigned to something inescapable, icy and mortuary.

"Not Rome, Rome doesn't have anything funereal, I hope you'll agree."

"I agree," said Zandel. "In Rome one can die with lightness just like in New York. The city doesn't notice who dies. In other words, one can disappear unobtrusively, incognito, without arousing surprise. And most of all without shame. There is something shameful in illnesses and even more in death. Luckily he who dies doesn't have time to feel ashamed, because death erases him and also erases his shame."

I kept feeling uncomfortable with these topics, which were completely unusual for us.

"It is the light that saves Rome."

"Light is substance, feeling, color, depth. Light corresponds to life, just like the schoolbooks say. Life. But do you realize that in those big interstellar spaces light travels in the dark? Light disappears in the void while its journey continues on at maximum velocity. It only becomes light when it runs into a solid body, a planet or else an asteroid. The big distances of the universe are measured in light years. But in reality, these might be called dark years. In other words in the big empty spaces of the universe there is only profound darkness, which remains dark even when it's crossed by light."

"One could say that darkness is always equal to itself, both in the spaces of the universe and in the hallway of our home. But actually it's not the case. In Rome for instance, the darkness is gentle. The sky is never black the way it is in the universe, or even in Helsinki or Saint Petersburg."

"Exactly, I wouldn't want to die in Helsinki nor in Saint Petersburg."

Perhaps these discussions of death had aroused him, because Zandel began to undress me, slowly as usual, to taste the discovery of my body. He kissed me bit by bit as he uncovered my shoulders my breast my belly my legs. I immediately took off my shoes and lay down on the bed. Zandel entered with sweetness, and then he made love with a desperate energy, as if it were a goodbye. Surely not. I had allowed myself to be influenced by those discussions. Perhaps it was his way of exorcizing his illness, which was not so serious to judge from the force with which he was squeezing me to the point of hurting me. It seemed he was digging deep within me, searching for extreme pleasure, a radioactive pleasure. It daunted me.

"You are crying."

"No, I'm not."

Zandel hugged me again, he held me tight in his arms for a long time, and he dried my tears with his kisses. In other words, we had plummeted into a romantic scenario, or rather into funereal eroticism. Even Zandel realized that we had acted out an excessively sentimental scene because, before he said goodbye, he resumed his usual behaviors, supported by a light smile, as if he wanted to convince me that those discussions about death were only an academic game. So I was finally relieved, in perfectly bad faith, from an afternoon of very deep despair.

On the street I immediately brightened up, and I stopped for a few minutes at the supermarket in Monte della Farina. I bought kitchen soap at random to justify my tardiness to Giano, just like I had done other times.

"You've filled up the house with soap," Giano said when he saw me arrive home with those boxes.

I smiled as a form of indulgence towards myself. So, Giano was not as distracted as I wanted to believe?

"If I had to ascribe a meaning to this accumulation of soap, I would advance the hypothesis that you have a subconscious desire for cleanness, for innocence."

Here we are, I said to myself, Giano once again plunges down into ridiculous exhibitions of tabloid-like psychoanalysis.

"My desire for cleanness has to do with floors, bathrooms, dishes and pots; not with my subconscious, please."

GIANO

I don't know what to make of a brief article that just came out in the Roman section of the *Corriere della sera*. It's someone's revenge. But whose? Why not consider it the likely case of a journalist who is simply opposed to my urban-planning ideas? Many of my colleagues, for example, couldn't put up with the uproar I had caused among the students, who preferred to come to my terroristic classes, leaving my colleagues' classrooms deserted. So some poison coming from the university could have settled on the pages of the newspaper.

"We can imagine that our urban planner's greatest joy would be a shower of smart bombs on certain neighborhoods in Rome like Parioli, which has triggered his destructive fury, but luckily only virtually." The article unfolded more or less in this sarcastic tone, but I have to admit it was well-informed about the blocks that my plan would eradicate to leave room for some small parks and, in proportion, tall trees such as pines or Roman holm oaks. It was all reported in detail. It is obvious that the journalist had made use of information obtained directly from some student who had taken my classes.

The article was not completely negative, because it granted that in a far-away future my theories could possibly produce excellent results in rebuilding the face of modern Rome. The issue of time entered my project forcefully: time as the future. "Not all times are equal and run at the same pace," Don Quixote says.

The article had an incredible effect on me, even though it was temporary. In substance, apart from the bothersome sarcastic excesses like the one about the smart bombs, I more or less agreed with the journalist from the *Corriere della sera*. Self-criticism or self-flagellation? Certainly the paradoxical excesses of my urban-planning proposals ended up amazing my students, but, most of all, spurred discussions and debates among them, which also extended outside the classroom and beyond the university. This was the sign of my success.

I've decided I will talk about this article in class, because I don't want my students to think that the journalist's sarcasm hurt my pride. I'm used to the hysterical reactions sometimes caused by my stances towards allegedly modern urban planning and architecture.

Lightning bolts rained down on me from everywhere at the university when I explained that Le Corbusier is primarily to blame for the horrific anthills built in all the suburbs of major European cities. The famous Ville Radieuse in Marseille — baptized by its inhabitants, among other things, as "La maison du fada," the madman's house — is the model that inspired the architects and surveyors who built the monstrous anthills of the suburbs. And it was again Le Corbusier who inspired the developers of those sun-catcher tract houses that disfigured so many seaside areas and even the countryside.

After the dinner to celebrate his return from New York, we didn't hear anymore from Zandel, or rather, I didn't hear from him, whereas Clarissa certainly will have seen him and they probably celebrated his return in bed.

CLARISSA

My God, I feel so sick. I stuffed myself with Xanax, but the superficial calm doesn't cancel out my deep apprehension. (I feel a certain resistance to speaking of anguish, even though this would be the right word.) My encounter with Zandel after he returned from the United States dragged me into a deep depression. (This is the diagnosis.) It's been two weeks since then, and I haven't received any messages from Zandel. My cell phone is silent, and his is unavailable.

Zandel's illness is certainly not viral pneumonia as he wanted us to believe that evening when we had dinner at his place. I know perfectly well for what illness you have radiation therapy, and I also know that radiation treatments are measured out in proportion to how bad it is. For this reason, the massacre of his red blood cells causes me to have heavy thoughts. Unfortunately, I can't talk about it with anybody, least of all with Giano. All I have is desperate thoughts in my loneliness.

This morning I tried to read a few more pages of Giano's novel. I was hoping that somehow it might be a distraction for me. Instead, it makes me uncomfortable every time, seeing myself pierced like an insect there on the pages that Giano distills with wickedness. It's almost a psychological distress, because it's hard for me to make Marozia and Clarissa coincide, and I no longer know whether I should be on this side or the other, whether to be anguished, pill-addicted Clarissa or Marozia, triumphant and unaware sinner. It's strange how in reality I still have some mental reluctance about committing my glorious adultery, whereas Marozia isn't even aware of her adultery. I'm almost a Catholic in my unconscious, whereas Marozia is a petty, erotic pagan, who doesn't know the subtle pleasure of sinning. It's a great Christian invention, sin, and that delicious feeling of guilt that accompanies the sinner.

I've realized that this book is difficult reading for me. It's a magnifying lens that distorts my image. The stories about my encounters with Zandel before his trip to New York are very well concocted, going beyond the facts. If I had read them in time, they would have given me a few useful suggestions. From these same tricks one can see that Giano made everything up, sometimes making his inventions coincide with reality, sometimes correcting reality or even anticipating it.

LUIGI MALERBA

Now my temptation would be to imitate Marozia, who is more serene, nonchalant and overall more cynical than Clarissa. Perhaps she's also more intelligent. His writing is a cruel joke, and all together it's also a little grotesque. So much confusion in my head because of Marozia, because of a ghost.

But I felt the greatest surprise after strenuously deciphering two more pages of the novel where Giano describes my encounter with Zandel after his return from New York. Here they are.

"I wouldn't want to die in Helsinki nor in Saint Petersburg," said Zurlo. "In Rome," Giano writes in his book, "one can die with lightness just like in New York. The city doesn't notice who dies. In other words, you can unobtrusively disappear, incognito, without arousing surprise. And most of all without shame. There is something shameful in illnesses and even more in death. Luckily whoever dies doesn't have time to feel ashamed, because death erases him and also erases his shame.

Marozia kept feeling uncomfortable with these topics, which were completely unusual for them.

'It is the light that saves Rome.'

"Perhaps," Giano goes on to write in his book, "these discussions of death had aroused him, because Zurlo began to undress her, slowly as usual, to taste the discovery of her body. He kissed her bit by bit as he uncovered her shoulders her breast her belly her legs. Marozia immediately took off her shoes and lay down on the bed. Zurlo penetrated her with sweetness, and then he made love with a desperate energy, as if it were a goodbye. Surely not. Marozia had allowed herself to be influenced by those discussions. Perhaps it was a way for Zurlo to exorcize his illness, which was not so serious to judge from the force with which he was squeezing her to the point of hurting her. It seemed he was digging deep within her, searching for extreme pleasure, a radioactive pleasure. It daunted her.

'You're crying.'

'No, I'm not.'

Zurlo hugged her again, he held her tight between his arms for a long time, and he dried her tears with his kisses. In other words, they had plummeted into a romantic scenario, or rather into funereal eroticism. Even Zurlo realized that they had acted out an excessively sentimental scene because, before he said goodbye, he resumed his usual behavior, supported by a casual smile, as if he wanted to convince her that those discussions about death were only an academic game. So she was finally relieved, in perfectly bad faith, from an afternoon of very deep despair."

Two, almost touching, pages that Giano wrote I don't know when. Perhaps before my encounter with Zandel? Is Giano writing his novel or my life, I wonder? Sometimes with a certain wisdom, I must admit, but this, conversely, increases my apprehension. Or is it me, Clarissa, who lives his novel through Marozia's unreality? If I wanted to recount my encounter with Zandel after his return from New York I would have used the same words that Giano used in his novel. This novel that started with a joke takes an incredible erotic and sentimental turn at a certain point when Giano describes my hypothetical encounters with Zandel.

Luckily, not so hypothetical.

I don't know what to think. I see that Clarissa is very absent minded. I talk to her, and she answers at random. We watch a movie on TV and, more than once, I realize that she's not following the plot, and her mind is who-knows-where. No news about Zandel except for the fact that he suspended his activity at the university. His office is managed by his colleagues, who are keeping up, among other things, with the work Zandel undertook on behalf of the city of Rome. In particular this includes the supply of public services, cobbled streets, squares and gardens for the two neighborhoods of Finocchio and Pantano, which in recent decades have developed with buildings that are ninety percent illegal. Zandel had told me about this project and about the work unfortunately subcontracted by two companies that ended up being totally unreliable. They didn't adhere to his technical documents, and in the end they might have jeopardized the prestige of his office.

Poor Zandel, in a moment of jealousy I wished he would drop dead, and now I feel virtually responsible for his illness and only wish him to get well, or in any case, not to die. For now.

Clarissa's behavior has recently gotten much worse. Not only is she absent minded to the point that it's become very hard to have a conversation with her, but now and then she's annoyed when she answers me. Yesterday I showed her the electricity bills that we have to pay in person because we've recently changed banks. She was offended.

"The queen of the gypsies."

"What have gypsies got to do with it?"

"Gypsy women are called queens to flatter them, but in reality they are forced to be bag ladies and provide lowly services."

"Paying the electricity bills would be a lowly service, then?"

"Very low and petty."

I didn't want to argue, but it's obvious that recently Clarissa is not thinking straight. She realized that I was worried, and immediately she retorted that I am a deviant. I don't understand what she means by this word.

"Nobody ever called me a deviant."

"I'm calling you one."

"What do you mean?"

"That your thoughts follow trajectories that lead to places beneath the level of the sea and the earth. To be clear, beneath the level of reality."

"Thank you for the really exhaustive explanation. I don't know whether I should be offended."

"Do as you will."

I don't know how to defend myself from Clarissa, who is depressed and now out of control. And so we have our first verbal confrontation face to face. Unfortunately it's impossible to go back and delete what has already been said the way you can delete what has been written on a computer: you highlight the lines, and with a click they disappear forever. Now I know that I mustn't surrender to the bad mood brought on by our words and this sudden sky of lead, the heavy air of an incipient Roman winter that confuses ideas and compromises the Order of Discourse.

But Zandel is clearly still at the top of Clarissa's thoughts with that mysterious (not really) illness and those poor red blood cells decimated by American radiation treatments. To judge by Clarissa, it's a bad illness. She is the one who immediately perceived the sign of danger. Every time she's the one who feels the pressure and the density of things. It's easy to foresee that Clarissa, a luxurious and resourceful woman, will soon manage to replace Zandel. I can also imagine that her choice will be an intellectual, an architect or a writer, a painter or a musician, depending on the opportunities and what's available out in the piazza.

CLARISSA

Zandel hasn't replied to my messages on his cellphone for fifteen days, and I can't talk to him because he's never "available." When Giano is not home I lock myself in the bathroom and cry for about ten minutes, then I splash my eyes with fresh water. These ten minutes of tears are better than Xanax. A relationship that kept my marriage with Giano alive has become my punishment, as if my love for Zandel was a fault and not a happy complement to my relationship with Giano, a profitable and innocent therapeutic adultery.

For a few years I considered my relationship with Zandel a pleasant distraction and nothing more, as I imagine Giano's relationship with Valeria to be, more or less. But I've now realized that I'm desperately in love. I was convinced that my desperation and tears were an enhancement of my love. Now, from a more distanced point of view, I feel I've fallen into a romantic and luxurious soap opera, the assigned place for sublime love. It's a trap with no escape.

Giano spends a few hours a day writing his book, and in the evening instead of television he resumes reading *Don Quixote* in the beautiful but bulky "Millenni" edition by Einaudi. I noticed that he doesn't use a bookmark, and every night he opens the volume at random, as if it were the Bible. I have to say that it's a very relaxed way of reading. It's a sign of confidence. Or is it disorder? I tried to read few pages of this big book, as well. The skies are wide-open, and there is a lot of light over there in the adventurous Mancha. I found it very relaxing, believe me. Certainly it's better than my usual medications.

Giano's words are coming back to my mind like a tingling beneath the skin: a sarcastic prediction and perhaps some involuntary advice to replace Zandel. An intellectual, Giano wrote in his novel. From this you can understand Giano's unintentionally high opinion of me and of my beauty. Perhaps he was influenced by Zandel, who saw me shining like a diva. Or maybe, it's complete bullshit instead, dictated by a secret, ultra-violent jealousy?

And Dulcinea, what does Dulcinea say?

GIANO

It seemed that Clarissa had given up on our trip to Strasbourg, but actually she hasn't.

"Since you've agreed to my request to go to Strasbourg together," she suddenly told me, "you should tell me when we can leave. Keep in mind that I'm happy with one day and one night."

This sudden return to the idea of Strasbourg is preposterous on Clarissa's part.

"Obviously, I prefer Saturday and Sunday," I said, "but there's no problem with the university in case you prefer two weekdays instead."

"I'd be happy to leave on a Friday, just like you did to go to the conference. We can stay in Strasbourg all day Saturday, and we'll return Sunday afternoon or in the evening."

I couldn't help but express my surprise.

"You have strange and clear ideas about this trip."

"Very clear."

That "very clear" had confirmed — but there was no need — that Clarissa wanted to punish me by forcing me to repeat with her the encounter I had with Valeria in Strasbourg.

I don't usually get bored with Clarissa. We always find things to talk about, leaving aside my urban planning and Italian politics on purpose. Those topics risk putting all my neurons into a state of turmoil every time I find myself involved.

On the flight there — we decided to fly by mutual agreement — we passed the time like two novice tourists, commenting on the ground down below and its marvelous yellow patches of rapeseed, green ones of corn, and brown ones of worked crop fields. We take turns at the window to look outside, while our worldly friends on the plane read, write or take notes without ever glancing at the view from above.

After a delicious hare stew at a typical Alsatian restaurant, we went back to the small hotel where Clarissa had picked a courtyard bedroom with no view of the cathedral, so as to avoid noise.

"Look! This is a super pedestrian area. After eight o'clock in the evening not even taxis can come in. There is no noise."

"And I don't trust it," Clarissa replied.

I knew that it was pointless to argue, so we shut ourselves up in the room, which overlooked a narrow courtyard. From a window across from ours, a television was croaking out commentary on a soccer game. Much worse than a window overlooking the road.

With the remote pointed at the room across, which had the same TV as ours, it was easy for me to switch the neighbors' sports program to a nature show: crocodiles and hippos. The two young men in the opposite room, surprised, changed it back to the sports program with their remote. Then I, after a few moments: crocodiles, hippos and rhinos once again. Naturally, we turned off the light in our room to avoid being caught. Clarissa was laughing hysterically, muffled and careful not to be heard. The two young men couldn't figure out what was happening, and they were beginning to get irritated. They were cursing, shaking the remote and banging their fists on the TV. And again: the match for a few minutes and then suddenly lions and giraffes. We went on with this joke until the two fools left the room, slamming the door, to complain to someone downstairs.

In the morning we went out. The sky was cloudy, of a bronze color, and a stifling cloak loomed over the city, as often happens in this region.

"A storm is in the air," Clarissa said.

"No way, it's just the sky in this city. It's the smoke that gives a gray color to the clouds, which are white where we live."

"Are there many factories in Strasbourg?"

"It's cigarette smoke. Statistics say that Strasbourg has the highest consumption of tobacco in all France."

Clarissa got the joke and smiled at my silliness.

I tried to drag her to the outdoor café in Rue des Juifs, behind the cathedral, where I had been with Valeria. There was no way. She wanted to go in the opposite direction, so we had a latte with excellent croissants in a café across from the Hotel de Ville. Apparently Clarissa chose a path with well jointed pavement to save her heels from the overly rustic cobblestones. Naturally, when we crossed the flower market I tried to buy her a bouquet of cyclamens, but Clarissa preferred a small bouquet of Parma violets, and she wanted to leave the market immediately because all those flowers, those mixed scents, reminded her of a cemetery's miasmas.

It was obvious that Clarissa had perceived my intention to have her retrace Valeria's footsteps to get back at her for forcefully dragging me to Strasbourg for the second time. But instead she wanted to stamp this trip with her own mark by refusing everything I proposed. Clarissa is endowed with a surprising intuitive intelligence, and in this case, she managed to mitigate all of my intentions to punish her. Well done.

We found ourselves in the sleeper car. Once again, we looked out the window at the melancholic landscapes of the night, the interiors of houses and the neon of signs, without ever talking about Zandel or Valeria despite our silent desire for conversation and confession.

The wheels spun rapidly on the railways. It was background noise for our silence while the train ran through the night.

Luigi Malerba

CLARISSA

I don't know if the trip to Strasbourg with Giano was a good idea. Overall, it was a boring trip, and Giano was in a bad mood. He was trying to make me sleep in the same room where he had slept with Valeria and her big ass, to take me to the same café where he had taken Valeria and her big ass, to give me the same cyclamens that he had certainly given to Valeria and her big ass. All this, in order to observe my reactions and compare them with those of Valeria, just maybe to discover some embarrassment in the eyes of the waiter at the café or the flower woman at the market. Assuming that they are gifted with an elephant's memory. How did I realize this? Giano was too confident. He is usually a dolt in such things, and he had an unnatural insistence on wanting to follow certain paths that he had already decided on beforehand. Perhaps my opposition contributed to his plummeting into Global Melancholy up in Alsace. Those are his words, and they correspond to his deep, secret mood. It's a submersed Atlantis that influences moods and gives rise to the darkness of his feelings. The only fun and happy moment was the joke with the remote control.

It seems that periodically, even during his classes at the university, Giano suffers from effusive breakdowns. During these the syndrome that he defines as Global Melancholy manifests itself. It's the only type of globalization that he recognizes. And on those occasions even his Urban Deconstruction appears to be useless to him. His political rage is useless. His polemic against pollution is useless. "Let even the particulate matter come," Giano wrote in his book in a moment of nihilist exaltation. "Come, carbon dioxide, particulate matter, benzene and all the other poisons. Come in droves. After all, particulate matter has already crept into our bodies and circulates in our blood. Let the industries go on spitting out carbon dioxide and dioxin, polluting the rivers, the sea, the sky, the aquifers, widening the hole in the ozone layer. Seveso, Mestre, Gela, Priolo, Chernobyl and Bhopal in India, where the American multinational Union Carbide, damned pesticides, produced a toxic cloud in 1984. Twenty-two thousand dead and no statement or trial for the culprit. Every year since then, the streets in Bhopal fill up with protesters who burn an image of Warren Anderson, the president of Union Carbide at the time of the disaster. It was the biggest environmental disaster in history."

Long gone are the days when Giano gave toasts in class with his students, ordering drinks — strictly Italian — for everybody to celebrate the bulldozers starting to destroy the monstrous cement skeleton of the Fuenti on the Amalfi coast. It was a good omen for the arrival of Urban Deconstruction. And finally the gigantic illegal condos of Punta Perotti on the Bari seaside disappeared under a huge cloud of dust. This was a little grain of nothing compared to all the illegal cement that was saved by the government's concession of permits. An ebb and flow of illusions and disappointments.

I took a glance at the last pages he wrote, and I found confirmation that in Strasbourg Giano wanted to force me to repeat the same paths as Valeria as a punishment. He wanted me to sleep in the same room, get coffee at the same café and accept a bouquet of cyclamens at the flower market, all just like Valeria and her big ass. Poor Giano, he's so naïve and so mean.

No, the forced pilgrimage to Strasbourg was not a good idea.

I opened the table drawer and resumed reading the notebook where Giano ironically foresees my next relationship with an intellectual, an architect or a writer, a painter or a musician, to replace Zandel. As if intellectuals could be found here and there passing by on the street corners. And according to him, would Clarissa have to position herself at a crossroads and grab the intellectual by the neck as he passed by? Go ahead and be ironic. It's not to be dismissed that I could really find him, perhaps an urban-planning architect like Zandel. It would serve you right, Giano, with your intoxicated irony.

I knew that one of these days it was bound to happen. To be honest I was hoping for it. I don't even know that student's name. While he was leafing through a book in Giano's library, I heard an ambulance siren from the street. I approached the window to see whether it had come to pick up some victim on our street. The student followed me, and he leaned against my body to look outside. I barely turned towards him, and we found each other face-to-face only a few inches apart. We looked each other in the eyes, and a second later we were hugging and kissing deeply without a word, while his sturdy arms were sweetly laying me on the floor on top of the rug. He got on top of me and then inside with infinite sweetness. A pause, and then I suddenly felt him sinking inside me like a pneumatic drill. I was jolting on the rug. I was discovering the pleasure of a fuck without the elasticity of the mattress, with my ass on the hard floor. It was a long bout of lust and finally two orgasms perfectly in sync and then total relaxation. We were exhausted and smiling.

We laid on the rug for I-don't-know-how-long. It seemed like the right amount of time to me, as right as his every caress and every kiss on my breast, which the young man uncovered with his already expert hands. I kept my eyes shut to prolong that sudden dream of love.

We got up without saying a single word but smiling with a sudden joy in our complicity over the fantastic game we had allowed ourselves.

I'm a whore, I said to myself as soon as I closed the door behind the student. Only a whore gives herself to a stranger in that way — a forty-year-old woman to a twenty-year-old guy. But how happy I was about that great fuck caught midair. It would remain my secret, stored deep in my memory forever. Deep in my heart, I should say. I don't know how, but while I was saying to myself you are a whore, you are a whore, tears started falling from my eyes. They seemed to be tears of happiness. I went to my bedroom, and I got undressed. I was naked, completely naked, and I lay down on my bed on my back. Just like that, for no reason. Or perhaps to use my imagination and prolong the orgasm from that marvelous and loving rape.

That student never showed up again in Giano's library. I wouldn't want his exams to suffer because of me. But every time I look at that rug, a beautiful, old red Bukara, I remember him with tenderness and languor.

And now, after this tale, I beg you not to seriously think I'm a whore.

GIANO

"Boycott the banks!" I admit it. I wouldn't be unhappy about boycotting banks. In this respect, I remember that Bertolt Brecht said that the person who establishes a bank is guiltier than the one who commits armed robbery of it. You'll have to excuse me, all of you mysterious naïve anarchist compulsive mural makers, but I really can't accept your invitation, or rather, I can't obey your command. I wouldn't even know where to start. This statement is of artisanal craftsmanship, written in capital letters in red paint. It appeared during the night, because I'm sure it wasn't there yesterday. I would have noticed it for sure when I came back, sprayed in such bright red on the wall of Via del Governo Vecchio, near the building where Clarissa and I live. As a side-note, it's a street where there aren't any banks. I wonder who can find such a statement useful and why.

Boycott the banks. Between you and me, no one can think they're going to get results by writing a statement like this on the wall of a street in Rome's Historic Center. According to them, this is supposed to be an example of political struggle: a message thrown into the crowd. Is it at random or in strategic locations? And what would the strategy be for Via del Governo Vecchio? And according to all of you, is somebody going to let himself be convinced to boycott the banks? But first of all, you should give me some instructions because even if I wanted to, I don't know how to boycott the banks. Where does one start? Or perhaps this imperative suggestion just represents the first cell of discursive thought, the zero degree of contestation, the first level of cultural stratification? No please, let's not talk about culture because these are primitive manifestations, the wild imperatives of the tribe. Let's not talk about culture, please.

Now I'm wondering who wrote this statement, what he looks like and how old he is. Is he a boy or an adult? He's a stupid white man. Why white exactly? A sixteen-year-old who shows up on his scooter, quickly paints his graffiti and takes off. But what does this sixteen-year-old know about banks? Perhaps someone commissioned the statement from him. Did they pay him? Who gave him the spray can? No way. He's a bearded thirty-year-old who wanders at night to dirty the walls with idiotic statements and thinks he's a revolutionary.

Clarissa doesn't see the Roman graffiti, or rather, she sees them but she refuses to see them.

"They dirty the walls. One ought to take them by the neck and make them pay for the cleaning, or else a large fine would do, one hundred euros per word. Or better yet, force them to lick the paint with their tongues."

"You are making it into an issue of city cleaning. Instead, I wonder who is interested in writing these imperative messages along the streets. We agree that nobody will start to boycott the banks, but this statement poses the question of the banks as a scandal, which is what those who read it perceive. Look, everybody, banks are not the peaceful institution you believe them to be. Instead they're a place for criminal speculation, recycling, swindling at the expense of the savers."

"Don't you think you're giving too much importance to a meaningless appeal written on a wall by some scoundrel? Fanciful anarchists and other outcasts of the earth will always be around."

I showed Clarissa the most preposterous of all these statements. A few days ago, it appeared in Piazza Navona on the right side of the newspaper-stand just past the café entrance: "Sew the animal's face with the human face."

"With all my good will," I said, "I can't find a meaning in these words. They're not even funny, not even realistic."

"You're looking for verisimilitude on the walls?" says Clarissa, who doesn't want anything to do with graffiti. "I don't even want to know what he had in mind, whoever wrote such a stupid invitation. Perhaps only air, emptiness."

"You're right, but ideas are not always a gift from the sky, and sometimes they can even be picked out from within foolishness."

"I think you're placing too much trust in Roman wall plaster to broaden your perspectives."

"You're right, it's a senseless stitching together. But sometimes nonsense can hide a gamble. I mean, even the wave probability function was a gamble."

"You are comparing some mural idiocy to the greatest paradox of nuclear physics."

"You are right. I beg Heisenberg's pardon."

CLARISSA

Zandel called my cell phone while I was with Giano at Nardecchia, the antique prints shop in Piazza Navona.

Giano was looking attentively at a marvelous perspective of the bridges over the Seine in Paris printed by Cheraux, I'd say at the beginning of the eighteen hundreds. It was a wedding gift for the daughter of our friend who works at the Ministry of Foreign Affairs. Every time Giano buys a gift it generates a bit of suffering because he almost always likes the gift, too. He would have been happy to keep this marvelous perspective of the bridges over the Seine for our own home, but all our walls are already filled with paintings, drawings and lithographs. And so we can no longer buy anything else for ourselves.

And suddenly my cell phone starts buzzing in my purse.

"Sorry, you've got the wrong number," I said as soon as I recognized Zandel's voice. I couldn't talk to him in front of Giano, damn it, and luckily Giano didn't notice that I had used an informal tone with a stranger who had dialed the wrong number. Poor Zandel! What rotten luck! He couldn't have found a worse moment. Poor Zandel, but mostly poor Clarissa. Really, poor Clarissa who deprived herself as soon as she recognized Zandel's voice. What else could she have done?

And now was not the time to show Giano my desperation. I hadn't heard from Zandel in almost two months, and when I finally got a call, I can't even talk to him. His cell phone always says that he's not available. It's clear that Zandel keeps his phone off, and this means, more or less, that he's refusing all communication. The voicemail isn't even activated to record a message. Who knows what he wanted to tell me with that phone call. I will never know.

Giano is all concerned about the statements written on the walls of Rome by unknown hands. Whether stupid or provocative, preposterous or simply banal, they nonetheless absorb his attention. Sometimes he talks to me about them, but I can't manage to take any interest in this phenomenon, which is dumb and sterile in my opinion. Conversely, he believes that those graffiti express the subconscious of the city, that they are the revelations of its subterranean drives, a sort of unconscious transference, as if Rome were lying down on the analyst's couch.

"More than subterranean drives they're a permanent Cloaca Maxima," I said, "which collects all the garbage of the Roman and barbarian subculture."

"The Cloaca Maxima runs underground, in Rome's viscera, in the dark while the statements, as preposterous as they are, flower in the light on the city walls and help us to understand what is brewing down underneath."

"A lot of shit," I said.

This is how the dialogue about graffiti ends.

And now I don't understand why Giano describes Marozia as having read *Andreas*, a book by Hofmannsthal, which, to tell the truth, I've never read, intimidated as I was by the name of that very difficult author. Perhaps Giano wants to improve the character of Marozia, to make her more interesting or more aesthetic? That leaves me with no other option than to read this book, so as not to feel inferior to the character that corresponds to me. To tell the truth, she's starting to stress me out with her smoky literary desires. Let's hope that Hofmannsthal's book won't be too boring, then.

This Marozia won't leave me alone. I met her in a dream. Sooner or later it was bound to happen. It was a strange dialogue, almost an argument, as if in front of a mirror. Marozia kept on talking, clear words and words that were blurry around the edges. There's a little bit of confusion, but in the end I can sum up the dialogue this way, just as I recall it in its fundamental elements.

"Can you promise me," says Marozia, "that the sheep is a catholic animal?"

"I can promise you nothing. On the contrary, I can tell you that I think you are talking a bunch of shit."

"Look, mister pope told me, and he knows about these things."

"Enough said, then. What do I have to do with it?"

"Are we friends or what? I'd like if we agreed on everything, sheep included."

"And why would the sheep have to be catholic?"

"Isn't the sheep the mother of the lamb? Practically the mother of the Agnus Dei."

I was irritated and uncomfortable.

"The lamb is the son of the sheep. What a great discovery? But God has nothing to do with it."

"So then, the sheep, the mother of the lamb, is in a parallel situation to that of the Virgin Mary."

"No way. This is blasphemy. I'll have nothing to do with it."

I summed up the words of the dream, which seemed very long. I tried to organize them to preserve their meaning, however odd it may sound. In my summary I didn't use capital letters, and I should even have eliminated the punctuation because in my dream there were neither periods nor commas. And now it's pointless to waste time trying to find meanings in a dream like this one. It stages a totally senseless and blasphemous situation provoked by Marozia, who made me uncomfortable during our encounter and still makes me uncomfortable now that she comes back to my memory. It's lucky that people are not responsible for their dreams. I can't even tell Giano about this one because I have to pretend to ignore Marozia with him, since I know her by reading his book in secret. The interesting thing for me is that in the dream I found myself face to face with my fictional alter ego. Something better could have come from this "epic" encounter between Clarissa and Marozia, but that's how it went.

Bad news about Zandel. A student of mine who occasionally works in his urban-planning office said that the architect goes to the Fatebenefratelli Hospital on Tiburtina Island once or twice a week for blood transfusions. His red blood cell problem is thus confirmed, but to me transfusions seem like an extreme remedy adopted when drugs no longer are effective. I didn't talk about this with Clarissa so as not to aggravate her anxious state of mind, which I can definitely attribute to Zandel's illness.

When she's depressed, Clarissa unloads herself by turning our apartment upside down. She called a decorator and had him put up new wallpaper in the dining room and the bedroom. Japanese paper in the dining room and a light blue moiré pattern in the bedroom. Naturally before giving the go ahead to the project, she showed me the wallpaper samples for my approval. But I knew she had already decided, and I was left with no choice but to approve her decisions and in addition to that, to show some sort of enthusiasm.

"This Japanese wallpaper is beautiful," I said. "It will almost feel like being in Japan."

"Japan is even further away than China, thank you very much," replied Clarissa, annoyed.

While the decorators were about to finish gluing the new paper to the walls, Clarissa took the opportunity of having lunch in the kitchen to ask me a question with an attitude that was just too distracted.

"Don't you think we should ask about Zandel?"

"Ask whom?"

"I don't know. He had some friends."

"Why do you say had? It's not like he's dead."

"He's been off the radar for several months. It's as if he were dead, or almost dead."

"I will try to find something out at the university, from his students or a colleague."

Clarissa seemed to calm down after my announcement and went back to watching the workers, who were gluing the paper rolls and then stretching them out over the walls.

"I've tried to call his cell phone," I said, "but he always has it off. It's clear that he doesn't want to communicate with anybody."

"A strange fellow, Zandel. He seemed to be a friend, and now he has cut off all contact."

"Why strange? He's sick, and everybody knows that certain illnesses change people. Sometimes they become irascible, and sometimes they hide away."

"Which illnesses? We can imagine what Zandel has, but it's not clear."

"We know for sure that he has an illness of the blood," I said, "because of those radiation treatments he had at the hospital in New York."

"Right, and why did they do the radiation treatments?" Clarissa's question seemed to already imply the answer.

"It's not hard to imagine. But now it seems he only has the problem with his blood."

"It seems to me like that's enough, don't you think?"

Clarissa quieted down, as if tucked inside her own tragic silence.

Poor Zandel, such an air of tragedy surrounds him, and perhaps in a month he will be here again, right in front of me, courting Clarissa or studying the sidewalks of London or Helsinki or Beijing. What kind of damn character can I extract out of someone like that? Let's forget about the sidewalks, but those red blood cells, that's really nothing to joke about.

But do Zandel and Irina fuck now and then? And what do his red blood cells say?

CLARISSA

When Zandel said he had a problem with his red blood cells due to the radiation treatments he had in New York, I understood everything. I forced myself not to understand and later to forget, but I no longer had any doubt about the nature of an illness treated with radiation. And after his reference to Chernobyl, our last encounter had taken place in an atmosphere of complete suspension. There was something unsaid between us, but we felt its presence. For my part, I felt the presence of the new problem with his red blood cells, but for his part, he felt something terrible that he was struggling to hide. So, I was trying to accept the fact that Zandel had started dying in secret. I wanted to decide not to think about it, to push it out of my thoughts, but that was impossible.

Giano gave me a small, Oregon satellite alarm clock — he explained to me that the brand, Oregon, is more or less the same as the brand, Omega, for traditional watches. The time is transmitted directly by satellite, which even takes care of adjusting for daylight savings time and standard time at the appropriate moment. It was a nice thought, so I can't tell Giano that I prefer clock faces with hands and hate these electric numbers. Moreover, to read them I have to press a button and the writing illuminates in a blue light that gives me the impression of nighttime even at noon. I believe he gave me this gift because I seem depressed to him. But it might also be that he gave a satellite alarm clock to Valeria and then, so as not to feel guilty, he gave the same one to Clarissa. I have nasty thoughts all the time.

The wallpaper in the dining room and in the bedroom has been changed, an elegant result that I couldn't care less about. Not at all. I was hoping to distract myself, but instead I realize that I've lost contact with things, including this beautiful and very expensive wallpaper. I can sit down in an armchair in the dining room and admire this wallpaper, which seems to be woven of fine straw and evokes the wallpaper of Japanese houses. And what does Clarissa care about Japanese houses?

I never miss a chance to get out of the house. I'm already tired of this expensive Japanese wallpaper, of the dome of Sant'Andrea della Valle, of the terrace overlooking the roof-tops of Rome, of the forest of television antennas and now of the satellite dishes that dirty the view of Rome like some Third World city.

To celebrate I don't know what, the Einaudi publishing house has, for the second time in about ten years, rented the loggias of

Castel Sant'Angelo. They offered everybody an excellent white wine from the Veneto, seafood and a background alternating among Mozart, Bach and Vivaldi. But the police helicopters continued hovering at a low level around the *castello*, their only evident goal being to ruin the party of a communist publisher with their deafening noise that covers the music and forces us to talk loudly. I feel a little ashamed of myself, but I started to check out who is around so as not to be left alone when Zandel goes where, sooner or later, everybody goes. At social events like this, Giano gives me all the freedom in the sky with no qualms. This is how, in Castel Sant'Angelo, I ran into the writer Lucci Nerissi, whom I barely knew. He took my hands, staring at me intensely, as if my presence struck him like a lightning bolt. There is a special way to look at a woman with desire — I don't know what to call it — with a desperate desire. Any woman of any age knows how to recognize this look, and she can react in a thousand ways or not react at all. But such a look is an event in and of itself. His look was serious, but his words were a gamble. Lucci Nerissi had immediately perceived my reciprocal feelings, and quite reasonably he took advantage of them. He invited me to go to Paris, speaking to me in an informal tone right away. A senseless and obviously playful invitation, and I enjoyed the game.

"I have a sudden desire that I want to confess to you. Come with me to Paris tomorrow, please. There's a Corot exhibition at the Grand Palais."

"Unfortunately, he's a painter I'm really not interested in."

"Overrated. Perhaps you are right," he said to me with a shrewd smile. "Then why don't we go out to dinner in Rome, tonight?"

"Another time. Now I have to get back to my husband."

I looked around to find Giano, who was a few steps away, observing me.

"Did I make a gaffe?"

"No."

"Can we see each other again?"

"Maybe."

"Do you want to leave all this to fate?" he asked me with a look of affliction.

"To free will, rather."

I said goodbye to the writer with a smile full of double-entendre. He couldn't come up with a response to my line, and he was left fixed in place and confused. I returned to Giano, who was talking to a young lady neither of us knew.

"Well, my dear," Giano said to me with a bitter smile, "do you realize you are behaving like somebody who wants to chat someone up? I can't believe my eyes."

"No, I'm not. Actually I'm behaving like those ladies who suffer from loneliness and who you might sometimes see at these society events. They look around hoping to meet a nice man for some innocent chit chat."

"Or for a brief erotic adventure, or even, why not, for a long erotic adventure. These are ladies willing to do anything, but who reserve the right to choose."

"Don't tell me you are jealous of that stranger."

"A stranger who said goodbye with a long hug. A stranger who doesn't seem to be a complete stranger."

"You think so? I don't know anything about him."

To tell the truth I didn't even know the title of a single one of his books, but for the moment I was not interested in his books. I can't deny that in some way I was smitten with Lucci Nerissi. Well, let's say that he had irritated me with his confidence, as if I was supposed to just fall into his arms like that. Moreover, I was bothered by his long and too-dark hair, his shabby outfit and the usual discolored jeans, like someone who wants to look like an artist at all costs. Anyhow I hope, I said to myself, he doesn't write poems. My God, I really wouldn't want him to be a poet. I don't know why, but poetry makes me uncomfortable. It makes me nervous. Moreover, with a touch of meanness, I recalled one of Feiffer's characters who was run-down and long haired just like him and who says, inside the cartoon: "I want to be a nonconformist too, just like everybody else."

In short, physically Lucci Nerissi earned a few rungs on the positive ladder, but on the other hand, for his demeanor he would plummet into negative territory. But let's just say that in men I never demand the golden ratio.

That's how I behaved with Lucci Nerissi: I was willing to tolerate his arrogance, who knows, as if he had struck my heart, or no, rather my viscera, in my stomach, so to speak. And this happened more or less right in front of Giano, who was so sarcastic and worldly, and as an affront to Zandel's memory. And now Zandel better not come and say that he couldn't give me a call after finding me unable to talk that one time. In the end, he's behaving like a man who's sentenced to death. There's nothing in the world more depressing than a man in front of you, face to face, with too short of a future, one closed off by a heavy gate with no mercy. Zandel began to show his weakness and mortality last time I met up with him, when we made love with a desperate fury after those funereal discussions.

Is Lucci Nerissi perhaps the intellectual ironically foreseen by Giano in his book? As far as I'm concerned, I would really say no, even if my gut is expressing some interest.

And Dulcinea, what does Dulcinea say?

LUIGI MALERBA

Giano

Who knows how he's participating in his illness, poor Zandel, what he thinks about it, what he tells himself when he's alone. Is he afraid? He certainly knows that he is kept alive by transfusions since his bone marrow doesn't produce red blood cells. Everything originated from a very widespread disease, which everyone struggles to call by name. In its most common forms it's called Neoplasm, in the most serious ones Death. Those terrible American radiation treatments killed the illness, but at the same time they almost killed the ill man by causing this disaster with his red blood cells. Cases of recovery from tumors are now a very high percentage, but in Zandel's case, it seems, the hematologist said, percentages are no longer worth anything.

Does Zandel know the risk he's running? Clarissa sometimes asks me about him, and I reply with the few things I find out at the university: almost nothing, but I didn't mention the blood transfusions to her. I called Zandel only once, but his wife told me he was sleeping (it was eleven in the morning). From Irina's cold silence I understood that she doesn't appreciate phone calls, just like Zandel doesn't appreciate visits.

Despite the discretion imposed by the Hippocratic Oath, the hematologist who is treating him openly talked with his colleague in the urban-planning office who was asking for news about Zandel for business reasons: little hope.

His colleagues at the university and his students talk about Zandel as if he were already dead: sorrowful faces, a few compassionate words, whispered comments, staring at the ground just like at a funeral. Poor Zandel, they killed you off before the time that was assigned to you, and the sad forgetfulness that obscures the memory of the dead has already started in advance. I will be forgotten for eternity, Zandel used to say to his students, who flattered him by saying that with his Sidewalk Urban Planning he would enter into the History of Urban Planning and even the annals of History. Laughing, Zandel would answer that even forgetfulness has annals and, in fact, forgetfulness even sinks into eternity by its very nature.

In my book every time that Zurlo comes on scene I am torn between pity and hate, as such I have to measure my words and not let myself get carried away with my cursing. My book is not and is not meant to be an act of vengeance or a settling of scores.

CLARISSA

I read *Andreas.* I found myself very involved by its mysterious and slightly funereal atmosphere as well as by the characters, who it seemed were all slowly being pulled into a whirlpool of decadent morbidity. Inside a big farm, the young protagonist misses the chance to fuck a young Roman lady, who offers herself to him on a big bed in the dark. What a silly man. And such a disappointment for those who read it. Would it have killed the author to let those two fools have a liberating fuck? They were ready to ignite like two matches.

The young protagonist arrives in Venice, and he moves as if drugged, against the backdrop of a depraved city where at night men wager underage girls in an improvised lottery. Overall, I like the novel, but unfortunately it was left unfinished due to the author's death. Anger and frustration, just like the absent love scene with the young Roman lady.

I can't understand why Giano has Marozia read this book. But perhaps there's not a specific reason. Often he too acts absent-mindedly, without giving a damn, so to say. No, actually attributing such intellectual reading to me must be an act of generosity. It's a gesture of love by means of Marozia. Why not?

But would it kill Zandel to call me? I don't think his wife keeps an eye on him twenty-four hours a day, and I also don't think he's incapable of dialing my number with his finger. It's clear that he just doesn't feel like talking to me: zero communication, and total despair on my part.

In his office, the secretary answers the phone.

"Zandel the Architect is momentarily away from Rome."

Why does he make his secretary say he's away from Rome if everybody knows he's been back from New York for more than three months and that he has serious health issues? Poor Zandel, I'm afraid that soon enough he will be completely away from Rome, and definitively so.

From long chats with Giano, I found out that Zandel goes to Tiberina Island twice a week, to the Fatebenefratelli Hospital for blood transfusions. Is he dying? In a certain sense we are all dying, but no doubt he is much more than Giano or I.

The first objective consequence of Zandel's illness is my loneliness. It was precisely that under-the-skin feeling of sin that made both my relationship with my husband and that with my lover more interesting. Giano understood the situation perfectly, and in his book he talks about my potential, probable future lover with a sense of irony but without scandal.

But why did Giano tell me about the blood transfusions? As an invitation for me to erase Zandel from my horizons? And consequently to find a replacement? No, this is impossible. It's only a vicious and morbid assumption on my part. Or is it my morbid and vicious desire?

Clarissa has been depressed for two months. (She insists that it's melancholy, which is a human feeling, while depression is a brutally clinical term.) She even went to our family doctor. He's a young fellow of good will, but he completely lacks that indispensable intuition that helps pinpoint a patient's problem and intervene with the right drugs. There really was no need to see a doctor to be prescribed two pills of Laroxyl a day, mineral salt supplements (Polase) and a cocktail of vitamins (Centrum). She had her blood pressure checked: ninety over fifty-six. It was a case of borderline collapse. So, Clarissa's psychic depression, which I attributed partly to the bad news about Zandel, is in large part a consequence of her arterial depression.

A few days ago, Clarissa almost attacked me, suddenly, during our morning coffee.

"One of these days, we will sit down and talk."

Right on the spot I was worried, but later I tried to react with calm to an announcement that sounded more like a threat.

"What about?"

"No, no, not now."

"Why don't you tell me the title? A conference, a debate, a book, a talk are all announced and presented with a title. That's all I'm asking of you."

"I wouldn't want to ruin everything with an announcement that would in any case be inadequate."

"You've already tried my curiosity. You know perfectly well that anything you have to say will arouse my full interest."

"A raw and honest title could worry you, whereas an articulated discussion following the laws of rhetoric and good manners could allow you to give me an honorable answer."

"Honorable? At this point if you don't tell me the title, I won't leave the house."

Clarissa reflected for a few seconds, and finally she fired her shot.

"Valeria."

I managed to stay calm. I answered with a smile.

"A good topic."

I said goodbye to Clarissa with a morning kiss, and I left home to go to the university. It was perhaps the first time that a topic referring directly to our personal relationships was put on the table, with the risk of interrupting our happy reciprocal ignorance.

I arrived at Piazza Navona with my head in flames. I got a lemon gelato to refresh my mind. I stopped to look at a poor mime all painted with silver glitter, including his face, hands and bare feet. He was standing still on a pedestal to perform I don't know what. The cape down to his ankles was perhaps meant to call to mind some ancient Roman character. But the silver? I tossed some change in the hat at the mime's feet, and I headed toward Via della Scrofa with the idea of walking at least up to Piazza del Popolo.

I wouldn't mention anything to Valeria before understanding what Clarissa had in mind about her.

I realize that my demand is preposterous. Zandel's illness has deprived me of many short vacations from my marriage. My marriage has thus become a suffocating place for me, just like a monad without windows, whereas Giano can count on Valeria, whose door is always wide open at any time of day. It's pointless to hide it: Zandel's disappearance from my horizons has created a serious imbalance between me and Giano. To restore balance to our marital situation, Giano would have to give up Valeria. Mine, however, is not a conversational request. I can only present it as a threat.

There's only one solution that might convince him to take heed of me: the threat of separation and then divorce. Giano loves me very much, and I'm sure that the idea of me abandoning him would throw him into despair. Unfortunately, I'm also in love, and I wouldn't despair any less than him. I could bluff, but I'm not cold blooded enough to manage such a demanding fiction. I should give him an ultimatum: either me or Valeria. And what if Giano chooses Valeria? Perhaps out of spite. He's totally capable of it. From the way he talks about her in his novel, you'd say he doesn't have much respect for her, but I know that he would not give her up easily. I'm tormented by this terrible dilemma: truth or fiction? Should I believe all the statements that Giano writes in his book? What I've read up until now approaches frighteningly close to the truth, and often the written situation anticipates or exceeds the real situation in which I, or better we, are enmeshed.

When I'm depressed I go to the salon or buy myself a new dress. There's a boutique behind the Pantheon in Via della Palombella where the young gay owner has always had the same taste as me, both for art-deco patterned fabrics, soft and wavy flowers, and for drooping, chemisier-like shapes. Everything at human costs. A dress on display in the window stopped me in my tracks on the sidewalk. Here's what shocked me: that dress was entirely similar, almost the same, perhaps the exact same as the one Valeria was wearing when I ran into her at the Lempicka exhibition at the French Academy. The silk was similar with its wavy diagonal stripes, which seemed to be drawn by the wind, the ruching workmanship was similar with its light wrinkles at the waist. I went back home with a bag that I immediately unpacked, and I put on the Valeria-style dress: a perfect provocation to welcome Giano.

Would you believe that he didn't notice anything? Not even that the dress was new. Since it seems impossible to me, I have to acknowledge that Giano is an impressive dissembler, in another words he's a clever bastard who always gets away with it.

I can't figure out what Clarissa has in mind. More than anything, proposing a conversation about Valeria seems to me like a provocation triggered by some loud-mouthed gossip that upset her. When I think how I always welcomed with irony Zandel's ongoing erotic-sentimental flirtations with her, I don't understand what new, evil spirit spurred her to challenge my patience on a sulfuric topic like Valeria. There was a tacit agreement between us that in our conversations neither Zandel nor Valeria could assume the role that they take on in our marital life. And then I really don't understand what sense it makes for her to parade around in a dress that is identical or almost identical to Valeria's. Is this a provocation? A joke? A metaphor? A quote? It is certainly an excessive gesture, which would require an equally excessive reaction from me. *Frangar* or *flectar*? I am in favor of *flectar*, elastic compromises rather than a fracture. Do doubts persist? At least on this point I will only have to agree with myself.

Ever since Zandel started to die, Clarissa has found herself off-kilter and on the verge of a nervous breakdown. I feel sorry about her nerves, but the problem is that if she loses control she risks putting our marital relationship into difficulty. That art-deco dress in Valeria's style seems to me as if it were produced by a lateral, divergent thought. It's a symptom of mental confusion. *Flectar*, certainly *flectar*, I repeated to myself. It's an idiotic, scholastic dilemma, like the buzz of a bumblebee, on which our marriage is being gambled.

But anyhow, after her verbal threat of a week ago, Clarissa has not since touched upon the topic of Valeria. The only wavering was in showing off that dress. Explicitly laying our problems out on the table will only lead to a dramatic consequence, and Clarissa knows full well what it is: it means opening the door to the Four Horsemen of the Apocalypse.

Well, whether Zandel is dying or not, I am a slut, because I went to the presentation of a book by Lucci Nerissi. I read the announcement in the paper, and I immediately decided to go to the Paesi Nuovi bookstore near Montecitorio where the reception was taking place.

I arrived in front of the bookstore's window already regretting having gone that far. I looked through the glass. There were about twenty people in total, almost all women, and two men sitting at a table in front of the audience — perhaps they were two presiders — and Lucci Nerissi was standing next to them. Like a falcon, he saw me through the window and rushed outside. He came up to me and hugged me.

"Do I have to thank free will?"

I smiled, happy that he remembered my line.

He took me inside the bookstore. My presence in that place meant exactly, almost against my will, that I was offering myself to him on a golden platter. I was so aware of it that I was already aroused by the predictable conclusion of that afternoon. I was wondering whether Lucci Nerissi had a place where he could take me, or whether instead a wife or other obstacles were in our way. At that point I had made my decision, and I just had to wait and see how he would manage the encounter.

To put it simply: I liked Lucci Nerissi. I liked him in a specifically physical way. I wanted to make love to him. I said to myself that betraying Zandel, who was so ill, was truly a colossal dirty blow. But I knew that a replacement — I didn't expect anything grand, just an efficient and pleasing lover — would perhaps save my marriage from shipwreck. Ever since Zandel's illness, our marriage had been sustained by a lazy, drowsy routine. I was so aroused that I forced myself to lessen the weight of the event: after all, I told myself, at the moment I was expecting nothing more than a fuck.

Giano is a great husband thanks in part to Valeria as a resource *extra moenia*, just as, up to that moment, I had been a great wife in part thanks to Zandel. The balance suddenly broke apart after his trip to New York, and then with his illness, which put him in parentheses definitively. Because of this, I was thinking about my marriage when I read a couple lines in the *Messaggero* that announced a presentation at the Paesi Nuovi bookstore in

Montecitorio of Lucci Nerissi's book, *The Suspicious Equilibrium*, about the risks of cultural manipulation. This is what I think I understood from the two presiders and from the words of Lucci Nerissi himself. And I thought he wrote novels.

What a beautiful voice, I said to myself, and I listened to his voice without paying attention to the words he said. What a beautiful voice. I understand how birds use their warbling as a means of seduction. Even elephants and crocodiles emit loud calls of love. Lucci Nerissi's voice was making me so horny that I was on the verge of having an orgasm right there in the bookstore. I talked about it with the wife of our pharmacist, who I often run into during my walks from Piazza Navona to the Pantheon. We share our secrets.

"Of course!" the pharmacist's wife said, and she told me about how she fell in love with her husband by talking to him on the phone and she betrayed him — only once, for goodness sake — with a singer from the chorus of the Accademia di Santa Cecilia. Obviously, I didn't reveal the name of my seducer to her, and most of all the seduction's second act. The pharmacist's wife, besides being an expert on eroticism, is an unbearable prude.

It really seems that there is no longer hope for poor Zandel. He's not suffering — in the sense that he isn't in pain — but it seems that he's so weak and depressed that he struggles to stand up on his feet. Every time I called, Irina told me he prefers not to see anybody because he gets tired. As a result, I had given up on seeing him, but finally, all of a sudden, Irina called to tell me that Zandel would be happy to see me. What could this be about?

I went to visit him at his house. He was very pale and dehydrated, but to tell the truth, he was pale even when he was fine. He even seemed to be in a good mood. He told me he didn't feel bad, he was not suffering, but he was always tired. It was a serious and total fatigue, he said, down to his toes. It seemed that his illness was fatigue, more the cause than the effect, or at least the cause and the effect of the disease at the same time.

"All this because of those son-of-a-bitch red blood cells," he repeated.

He didn't tell me about the transfusions, and obviously I didn't talk about it either. His wife had warned me that it was better not to talk about work either, unless he was the one who chose it as a topic of conversation. What on earth could we talk about? For the first time since we'd known each other I had the feeling there was something different about Zandel, as if his personality had undergone a change. There was the whiff of something different about him, and I thought that a serious illness like that causes changes in a person's substance. Those continual transfusions of strangers' blood: here was the true reason why I struggled to recognize Zandel in the way he was appearing to me now, after many years.

Now something strange had crept into his voice, into his faraway and disoriented eyes. He was still Zandel, sure, but a diluted and confused Zandel, perhaps precisely because of all those transfusions, all the strangers' blood that was running through his veins. I was aware of the absurdity of such a thought, but can't it perhaps happen that in absurdity there is sometimes a nibble of truth? Who were his blood donors? In Zandel's shoes I would have certainly wanted to meet them. Men or women? Italians or foreigners? Northerners Asians Africans? Perhaps also some scoundrels? Isn't there a risk of transmitting some bad germs together with the red blood cells? Obviously one cannot ask blood donors for a certificate of good behavior. I don't know whether Zandel had these worries, for blood was a prohibited topic during our meeting.

We talked about the university with a brief tangent of gossip, and in the end, to fill a sudden silence, I thought about turning to one of my usual expedients that Clarissa detests. But she wasn't there this time, and not even Irina's presence would interfere. Rather than a little story, I decided to present him Aub's paradox, hoping to conquer that silence and revive his attention.

"You have two parents," I said, "and in turn, both your dad and your mom had two parents. Let's sum them up, and by stepping back one generation we've moved from two to four units. Each of the four in turn had two parents, and in two generations, counting backward, we've reached eight units. Let's proceed backward from generation to generation. Each of the eight ancestors obviously had two parents, and we are at sixteen units. From sixteen we arrive at thirty-two, and from thirty-two we arrive at sixty-four. Even if we calculate in a few mishaps in deficit for each generation, where does the backward process lead us?"

Zandel looked at me, perplexed.

"Like Zeno's paradox in reverse," he said. "Whoever moves in one direction always has to arrive halfway up the path ahead of him before reaching the final destination. In conclusion, the protagonist will never arrive at the end because there will always be halfway to be covered ahead of him. Therefore, the path he walks becomes infinite. This is the real meaning of Zeno's paradox, the invention of infinity, or if you will, of immortality. Whereas your paradox goes back in a geometrical regression ad infinitum, and instead of arriving at Adam and Eve, alone in Earthly Paradise, it hypothesizes a planet that is more and more crowded. These are the tricks of logic. It sometimes goes off track and upsets our fragile reality. Luckily man is not subjected to the strict rules of logic. The unforeseen governs all human histories, and only on the unforeseen can we pin our hopes. As you probably understood, I would welcome Zeno's paradox with enthusiasm in its hypothesis of immortality, but I prefer to seek refuge among Lucretius's faction and wait until a *clinamen* takes place in my favor."

The parallel between the two paradoxes seemed inaccurate to me, but I didn't show my doubts. Zandel was speaking for himself, as if he were saying that his little hope would have wanted to welcome Zeno's infinite hypothesis, but then it turned towards an improbable but possible rupture of the logic of facts. And the facts were relentlessly proceeding in the direction of his death, with the sole exception, which my unhappy friend had openly expressed, of a future *clinamen*.

The discussion had thus become personal and uncomfortable. At this point I would have wanted to change the subject and ask him, for instance, how his projects were going during his absence. But I knew from Irina that he was highly distressed precisely by the fact that he couldn't even keep up with the work that was already underway.

I had learned that in Amsterdam they had accepted his proposal to increase the number of sidewalks that were protected by bollards — or Amsterdammertjes, as they called them. They had already been implemented in large areas of the city. They had essentially eliminated parked cars from almost the entire city center, to great praise from the pedestrian citizenry. They had tried to exorcize the drivers' rage by selling little chocolate poles. A brief hint at the little chocolate poles and then I hit the brakes hard because, following Irina's orders, we were in the area of prohibited topics.

I couldn't understand why Zandel had shown any desire to see me. Perhaps a goodbye? Excluding professional topics and obviously his health, we no longer knew what to say to one another.

"How is Clarissa doing?"

A surprise question.

"She's well, well enough."

Another prohibited topic, that of Clarissa. Should I have perhaps told him that she was depressed and holding on by swallowing a large quantity of anxiety pills?

At this point I stood up, and we ruefully said goodbye. Throughout our meeting, in Zandel's every word, in his every gesture, his approaching end seemed to be implied. It had now been several months that Zandel's life on death row was dragging on. I already knew before seeing him that a dialogue with a man sentenced to death has no prospects. The thought came to me that, overall, it was a literary meeting, novel-like. But how shameful to think about my novel on that almost funereal occasion.

"See you," I said to normalize my goodbye, knowing full well that our seeing each other again was an entirely precarious hypothesis.

"See you soon," Zandel said with a strange smile.

Soon? Where? Those were the thoughts that came to me.

Lucci Nerissi's office was on the second floor of a quite run-down building in Vicolo della Stelletta, a short street that crossed Via della Scrofa. Comfortable stairs lit by unpleasant neon lamps. We walked into the semi-darkness of a small room with a rustic Louis XVI coffee table from Parma in the center, a small bookshelf on the wall across the room and a big couch on the left. Books were scattered a bit all over the place, even on the floor. A lot of books. You could glimpse the bathroom through a half-open door. Everything was very clean amid the disorder: polished wooden floors, a big window hidden by a thin curtain that allowed the street's little bit of light to filter in.

As soon as the front door was closed, Luccio, as I decided to call him, led me to the couch. He hugged and kissed me, all the while trying to make his way with one hand so we could make love just like that, fully clothed, right there on the couch. I was shocked at first, but then I allowed myself to become overwhelmed by desire. A violent and brutal fuck. I didn't imagine I would take so much pleasure in being subjugated to the sexual violence of that stranger on that couch in that room where I had just set foot for the first time only a few minutes before. My body desired that encounter, and now it was satisfied. When I revived myself from the sultry vapors of my orgasm, Luccio began to undress me. I quickly found myself completely naked, and then he, too, rapidly undressed. We embraced one another lying on the couch.

"I like your skin. I like to touch you," he said, and meanwhile he was kissing every part of me and provoking new tremors with his tongue. But if he really likes my skin so much, I thought, why did he want to make love with us both clothed? But then I was partly compensated for the initial unease since we were together, touching and kissing each other, finally naked.

On my way out of Luccio's office, I had begged him not to accompany me because I am a married woman, after all. So, I left all absorbed in my thoughts while one flew to poor Zandel. He was solidly established in my subconscious, and now he was also betrayed. I am a slut, a double slut from the moment I stopped even feeling sorry about being one. But I wasn't so sure about my thoughts.

I walked looking down, treading carefully, making sure not to ruin my heels on the gaps in the cobblestones.

Punctual as revenge, when I returned home I found a huge box of chocolates delivered by courier to the maid. Stuck in the wrapping was a note with only three words, "As many thoughts," and, as a signature, a *Z* like the one in *Zorro*. So Zandel had decided to communicate with me by means of those chocolates. A childish idea with the risk that Giano would intercept the box. I wanted to hear his voice on the phone so badly, and what does Zandel do? He sends me a box of chocolates.

I counted them. There are sixty chocolates, which makes, according to Zandel's proposal, sixty thoughts. A request for my thoughts, I imagine. And then? What happens after the sixtieth thought? I put chocolate number one in my mouth, and then I hid the box under the wool scarfs in the wardrobe with my clothes. I'm still offended because Zandel denies me his presence on the cell phone, and I don't know whether I should also be offended by this ridiculous attempt at communication or whether I should welcome it as a paradoxical and fragmentary message.

The first thought with the first chocolate is that the arrival of this box managed to make my fuck with Luccio go awry. A perfect result from Zorro's point of view.

GIANO

Recently Clarissa has been talking in her sleep: confused and alarmed words as if she were at sea during a storm. She tosses in bed, kicks, complains about the wind that takes away her clothes and asks for help from a *luccio*, a pike. It is not clear where the pike pops out from, but perhaps I misunderstood. She seems to be suffocating in her sleep, she talks to the pike about her clothes, which have been torn off and lie fallen at its feet, and you could say that she ended up naked, as if the memory of the nudist village in Corsica had reemerged in the storm. Or perhaps the memory of Sandro Botticelli's Venus who rises from the waves. She gets mad at her clothes. Perhaps they disappear into the deep waters and are nibbled by fish. She casts her impossible curses all in the subjunctive. Clarissa uses the subjunctive even in her dreams. She's a classy woman.

It rarely happens that Clarissa talks in her sleep, but recently there's something bothering her, and she's started talking at length almost every night in confusion. Let's say that between us there are some taboo topics. These are like anti-personnel mines — anti-men and anti-women — that are scattered along our path, and neither of us wants to get blown up. We talk to each other, but we avoid politics and topics that are too personal. Each of us maintains a free trade zone that remains outside of the conversation and the other person's life. There are only a few communal problems. For instance, during the first years of marriage we had the problem of the children for whom we uselessly waited. We had even chosen the names for the son and daughter we had planned, Agostino and Alice. There was no particular reason for those names. We had simply picked them out of the wave of our imagination. After the disappointment and suffering, we felt like a couple as sterile as the sands of the Sahara, and this had an enormous influence on our relationship. I don't want to judge whether it is good or bad. Certainly the frustration was never openly confessed, but it was rooted deep, and — I'm also speaking for Clarissa here — it produced a subtle breath of freedom, actually no, of unscrupulousness, in our relationship. After those first years of useless waiting, we erased the problem, and we never talked about it again. We removed it completely.

Another night of agitated sleep for Clarissa brings a new nocturnal chat. It had been years since Clarissa last talked in her sleep, and this is the third or fourth time in a short span. I don't know whether these nocturnal apprehensions have by chance something to do with Zandel and his illness, which actually has a real impact on us. Anyhow, in the confusion of her nocturnal expressions, as far as I know, Clarissa never pronounced Zandel's name. Prudent even in her sleep, that girl.

It's normal that every change in the life of a person or a family causes small traumas that we don't notice but in a certain sense act in the dark, which is to say in the subconscious, which is to say in our dreams. Certainly Zandel visited Clarissa's dreams, even if she didn't pronounce his name in her sleep. Zandel was for us a habitual visitor, and so we felt his absence very much. We will feel it even more when the poor fellow goes there, where everybody goes.

"Zandel's absence is very strongly felt."

This was my gamble to test the ground.

"I think we will have to give up and try to forget him."

"Perhaps one of our best friends, but overall a boring man. Perhaps we needed his boredom."

"There's stupid boredom, and there's smart boredom," Clarissa immediately shot back.

"Sure, smart boredom. It could seem like a contradiction, but in reality it's an oxymoron, a very sophisticated rhetorical figure."

"Oxymorons also exist in nature," Clarissa pointed out. "For example, stupid men with a smart face, or smart men with a stupid face."

"Whom are you referring to?"

"You're so suspicious. No, no, I'm not referring to you or to Zandel. I was just saying it in general, and I could come up with famous names included in the two contrasting groups."

"One day we'll sit down and start coming up with names, beginning with Picasso."

I haven't understood what Luccio has in mind, what thoughts. I haven't even tried to read any of his books, but I already know that they are far from my interests and curiosity. Much affection, many compliments, words as resonant as bells with that beautiful voice of his, but no news about his life, his work, his neurons. My only experience, that of his hormones. I barely succeeded at getting him to say that he's married, but complete darkness on his relationship with the wife, on his political ideas, his allergies and idiosyncrasies. He must be one of those men who don't talk to women, who think it's a waste of words. I don't know what to think, whether ours is only a physical relationship or whether there's something else. I don't want to use the word that in these cases is used plentifully in novels because I don't think it's the right occasion. We're far apart.

The other night I had an anguishing dream, which fortunately went on to end gloriously with a great fuck. I'm on a small sailboat in the midst of a furious nighttime storm, in the company of Luccio, who is trying to keep the fragile vessel balanced. It soars on the waves and then falls heavily onto the black surface of the nocturnal sea. I'm holding on to the boat's mast, and every surge rips off my clothes, which can't withstand being hit by the water, and in the end I find myself completely naked. Luccio is at the wheel, and I call him to come to my rescue. Luccio finally arrives, he picks me up and takes me under the deck in front of a big stone fireplace where big wood logs burn with a crackle. Luccio lays me down sweetly on the rug in front of the flames of the fireplace, then he gets on top of me, his clothes still soaking wet, and just like that we make love, warming ourselves in front of the fire. Finally, only after we've made love, Luccio starts slowly undressing with grand gestures as if he were performing a striptease, and he tosses his clothes one after the other toward an imaginary audience. I'm a bit annoyed: first of all because Luccio wanted to make love wearing his clothes soaked with salt water, and then because of his exhibitionism. Conversely, it seemed completely natural to me that under the deck of the small vessel there was a big stone fireplace alight with a fire.

I've decided that I must be happy to have met a man whom I like, even if he goes on wanting to make love with his clothes on, even in my dreams. I think it's a need of his because when he's naked and feels somehow obligated, his desire probably crumbles.

It seems that this often happens, and that's why many men make love on couches, on the floor, in the car, in the bathtub, on tables or standing against the wall. The pharmacist's wife, who is a real encyclopedia of every erotic skill, explained this to me.

With Zandel, I used to talk, and he too used to talk, and there was Giano's involuntary cooperation during the recurrent encounters at our place, at the restaurant, at university ceremonies, at art shows, at book presentations or other cultural occasions. My husband had an academic and virtual sense of Zandel's sentimental or erotic fictions regarding me. For the two of us, who knew the truth hidden behind those fictions, they had a completely different sense. It may be that over time Giano has arrived at the truth — that's what it looks like from what I've read in his novel thus far. However, it's a truth that is not convenient to unmask, since he, too, has a skeleton in his closet — I don't mind comparing Valeria to a skeleton, despite her big ass.

If I managed to introduce Luccio to my husband, if perhaps I managed to make them friends, or nearly, then I could maybe hope for us to have frequent get-togethers. This would normalize my relationship with Luccio by way of an external guarantee from Giano. In other words, replace Zandel with him.

Luccio would be happy to take me to Barcelona for three days, where he's been invited to a conference on "Europe, Tradition and Progress."

"It's such a generic topic," he said, "it won't engage me much because you can say anything. But I already know that we will end up talking about topics beyond Europe, about Bin Laden, Iraq, Bush, and about the growing Anti-Americanism all over the world."

Giano told me more than once that conferences are occasions for a lot of chitchat and easy extramarital adventures for the delegates. Who knows whether Luccio considers me an easy adventure for a short time or something else? I don't think it's worth brooding over. From my point of view, catch a pecker in flight and that's it, as the pharmacist's wife says. It's useless to hope for another Zandel.

I've never been to Barcelona, and I'd be happy to go, if for no other reason than to see those porno pinnacles of Gaudí's Cathedral of the Sagrada Familia, the most spectacular phallic exhibition in Catholic Spain, but most of all to sleep with Luccio for two nights in a real bed. But what do I tell Giano? Barcelona?

What do I have to do in Barcelona? Among other things I know that Giano hates the standardized urban planning in the Olympic neighborhood and that, anyhow, he knows Barcelona well enough not to go back to it. This is all fine with me, but I can't find an excuse to go by myself to that city, which people tell me is very beautiful. I passed by the bookstore in Piazza Colonna, I bought a photography book about Barcelona, and I got Giano to find me, sunk into the couch with that book in hand.

"Why this interest in Barcelona?"

"A girlfriend of mine is going to Barcelona in a week, and she asked why don't you come as well?"

"A new friend?"

"New. I met her at the beauty salon last week. She'll be the secretary at a social sciences conference that will take place in Barcelona. She's a new friend."

"And what if I took a couple of days off and came too?"

"If only. Why not?"

I felt the blood in my ears run cold when Giano proposed coming to Barcelona with me. Nothing to be frightened about. I would have gotten out of it at the last minute with any old excuse, but I was convinced that he would give up on it in the end.

A trip is trial by fire for a couple. A trip, even a short one, with Luccio could be the confirmation of our relationship or its failure. This was a risk I was happy to take, and with optimism. Honeymoons, I said to myself, are a way of living together and studying and touching one another outside the usual environment, but they ought to be taken before marriage and not afterwards. You know how many mistaken marriages would be avoided.

For the moment I told Giano you don't know how happy I am that you are coming to Barcelona with me. What a hypocrite I am. I have him hook, line and sinker.

GIANO

I will take advantage of Clarissa's trip to Barcelona to finally see Valeria in peace. We will go to the Casina Valadier for happy hour with a panoramic view of Rome, then to a restaurant in Trastevere with a Roman guitar in the background or perhaps to Fregene for a good shrimp and calamari *fritto misto*, and finally to her place in Prati, Via Properzio, third floor, with the elevator.

Instead, we saw each other at the Ruschena Café on Lungotevere to breathe carbon monoxide and lethal particulate matter. We bought some sandwiches with prosciutto and cheese and two beers. At home Valeria had an abundance of fruit, and she also took care of the coffee. It was a small home that I was familiar with, converted from an apartment that had been divided into two. It thus had a very big bathroom, which must have once been the master bathroom, and a kitchen that was also very big, out of proportion to the house. The bedroom had only one window with double glass that deadened street noise, blue wallpaper and a low bed, a Japanese futon, an old acquaintance of mine. At last, I calmly observed the place that I had seen many times in a rush, with eyes only for Valeria.

I had been to Strasbourg with her, three days of ease and a low-key Kamasutra in the small hotel's bed, but it was the first time that I spent an evening and a night at Valeria's place, a homey evening, a fast supper, a little television jam and finally to bed.

Valeria was a woman full of horizontal fantasies, but I barely knew her standing on her feet. And for the first time, I had the chance to see her place for a whole evening. Old-fashioned furniture and rugs, it was the respectable and slightly sad portrait of the proper bourgeoisie that framed an improper woman. This was an aspect of Valeria that had escaped me during all our encounters dedicated purely to sex, during which she showed the attitude and confidence of a classy woman of the world. In the intimacy of her household though it seemed that everything was crumbling around her despite the display of some nice furniture or silverware and lithographs of painters who were almost too well-chosen, from Magritte to Mirò, from Capogrossi to Schifano.

Maybe I'm exaggerating, but that idiotic evening was a wholly negative experience. I couldn't really understand what wasn't working. Her past, which she herself defined as "naughty?" Or the present, "condominium" state of things? How could I ever live with a woman like Valeria? Even her life transpired in small episodes lived like adventures, almost always with married men. Over forty, bachelors no longer exist, and those few left are the refuse. Given the occasion, a one-night stand and move on, just like in the sleeper car with Morpurgo. It was a melancholy life without awareness of the melancholy, which is a noble feeling that is elegant in a certain way.

The idea of spending an intimate evening with her at her place was a mistake. It would have been much better for me to stay at home during those two days of freedom and write a few pages of my book. It was starting to thrill me because I could make the people move like puppets, people I live with and often see, whereas in reality I'm often a passive victim of situations. The novel gave me a feeling of power, almost of omnipotence, and if I had some hesitations in deciding the destiny of my characters, I attributed it to my inexperience as a novelist.

Let's say that I'm not lacking for material, and I must confess that I feel a certain satisfaction in using my writing to free myself of the many obstructions that hinder my thought and confuse my ideas.

CLARISSA

The Hotel Colòn, which is how they say *Columbus* in Spanish, overlooks the cathedral square, the noblest square in Barcelona. Throughout the entire first day, Luccio stayed at the university to listen to his colleagues' presentations. I slowly wandered around the cathedral on foot, but without going inside. The interiors of churches shock me because with all the sins I have on my shoulders, which is to say, on my conscience, I imagine that right there God's waiting in ambush to cast bolts of lightning at sinners. Then I returned to the hotel. That evening we went to bed early after a light dinner. This time we finally made love naked in bed. Finally. Four orgasms.

The next day Luccio was going to deliver his talk and then take part in a public discussion. He preferred that I stay at the hotel, and I, too, preferred it that way.

We got up at nine and had breakfast at the hotel, then Luccio took a taxi to the university. In the meantime in the square, some musicians sitting on the cathedral steps had started playing a folk motif with shrill trumpet blasts. At first, as if summoned from the urban wilds, two men and three women showed up, put their bags down on the ground and started a circular dance, jumping in time to the music under the white Barcelona sky.

In the meantime, the music was drawing more people, and everybody put their bags and hats down on the ground and started to dance around in a new circle a little further away. At this point I went up to my room because I was sure that it was better to see the dance from above. The improvised performance was a marvel in its perfect concentric movements, a dizzying spin on the thread of a folk jingle in the most beautiful square of old Barcelona.

The improvised circles were widening as more dancers joined in, leaving their bags in the center. And more circles were still forming in the open spaces of the square. What a fantastic game, what a beautiful surprise for Clarissa who had arrived from Rome under the Barcelona sun. How many thoughts and how many sudden whirlpools. How much confusion in my poor head.

I asked the hotel director for information. He told me that the "Sardana" is a very old dance that people do in the springtime in many of the squares of Barcelona. But also in other Catalonian cities. It starts with the music of these small folk orchestras that go and set themselves up along the sides of the squares, and in a short time spontaneous rings form, and they multiply until they take up the entire square.

This performance had sprung up just like that, as a surprise right before my eyes, and it had triggered a strange apprehension in my heart. Once again I had associated this feeling with poor Zandel who, while I was enjoying this performance in Barcelona, was perhaps dying. And now I was there with Luccio, a completely different relationship, composed of only a few words but said with the most sensual voice I had ever heard, finally naked in bed in this Spanish hotel named after Christopher Columbus.

This dance, which was so old and distant, had thus awakened a great, melancholic tedium within me — something similar to Giano's Global Melancholy. It leads me to swallow a Xanax pill every time. Xanax always numbs me without erasing my melancholia. Unfortunately I didn't bring this dishonest drug along in my bag with the facial cleanser, lotions, toothpaste and hair brushes. And so I'll be stuck with my apprehension, which does not counsel me to go out and look for a pharmacy while, in the square of the cathedral, Barcelonian men and women dance in the Sardana in a circle with the vast and breathy sound of the small orchestra. I would like to join them, but I don't have the energy. Moreover, what does Clarissa have to do with the Sardana? Would you believe that I would have wanted to be one of those women who dance the Sardana in a circle in the oldest square in Barcelona? Lucky women of Barcelona, lucky them.

Giano

I will confess that I endured Clarissa's absence with anxiety and disorientation. As a sheer marital fiction, I had told her that I would go to Barcelona with her, but then I thought that it would have been good for her to take a vacation far away from Rome and far away from me. Clarissa had offered me the chance of a vacation in her company, and I foolishly refused. It sometimes happens that I am incapable of choosing and then of justifying my behavior. My thought: taking a trip makes bad relationships worse, but it solidifies and improves good ones. Is my relationship with Clarissa good? Of course it's good, therefore I made a mistake by not going to Barcelona with her.

I got a phone call from Zandel's wife — I was about to say widow. My immediate thought was bad news. Instead Irina requested, with many excuses, that I give her husband back *Non-European Roots of Mathematics* by George Gheverghese Joseph because Zandel was studying calculations of area by the Egyptians and Babylonians.

But why didn't he call me himself if he wanted me to return that book?

"I'm happy that Zandel has resumed working."

"It's not really work. He's so bored, and he's looking for an excuse against boredom, but I believe that he's dealing mostly with incommensurable ratios in ancient geometry before Pythagoras, or so I think I've understood."

I didn't know what to say, nor did I want to be dragged into a discussion with Irina about incommensurable ratios. Moreover, there are mathematical topics that do not pass through a phone line. I knew from old disclosures that Zandel was pursuing an idea he had about unreal numbers, but I never understood exactly what he meant. I knew he was in search of something in the region of India and Mesopotamia and that he could make use of Gheverghese's book, with its ample chapters on Indian mathematics, precisely for this, rather than for the calculation of areas.

"Mathematics can be a resource. I will bring it to him tomorrow. It'll be an excuse to see him."

"It's better if you leave it with the doorman, because he still doesn't want to see anybody, not even friends."

"But he's doing better."

"No, he's the same as always."

"I will leave the book with the doorman, then."

"Thanks."

"Give him my best wishes."

"Sure."

The phone call was so cold that it seemed to have been taken from a freezer. I believe Irina was still annoyed about the compliments that her husband used to pay to Clarissa not only in my presence, but also in front of her. Between you and me, perhaps for this reason, most of the time Irina wouldn't participate in her husband's social life, and she viewed friends like us — we who were somehow involved in those ridiculous social rituals — with suspicion. And now the illness.

Unhappy Irina.

CLARISSA

A bit of a dark side in a man enhances his charm. Giano has many dark sides, together with an entanglement of magnetic fields that produce subtle apprehensions. First of all, he has almost completely erased his personal past, both remote and recent. There's a void behind him. When he returns home at dinnertime, I never ask — it's my first thought — where he was. He sits down at the table and barely eats. It's obvious that he has already eaten, but I'm careful not to ask him where he had dinner and with whom.

As far as mystery is concerned, Lucci Nerissi is also a champion. I didn't even get to know him during the trip to Barcelona. We sleep together, but as far as familiarity is concerned, zero. During the plane ride he sat in silence, and he barely answered my questions with a few distracted monosyllables. I thought he was afraid of flying. It can happen, and it's not the end of the world.

Men usually love to talk about themselves. Not Luccio, even less than Giano. It almost seems like he's got something to hide, and this excessive secrecy makes me uncomfortable, as if I had a relationship with a ghost with no identity and no life to talk about. In other words, I wonder who this Lucci Nerissi is, whether he has his own life, a past and a marital status. (I discovered that Lucci Nerissi is a pen name.) To make up for it, in the hotel in Barcelona he didn't presume to make love wearing his clothes. It was a solemn erotic progress that my hormones were impatiently awaiting. Many orgasms.

I'm insatiable, I realize that. Am I perhaps a slight nymphomaniac?

Giano

I met up with Valeria at a small café in the shade of the pine trees at the highest entrance to the Parco di Traiano, where the Domus Aurea is located — to be precise, at the top of Oppian Hill. Valeria wanted to meet up at that café because she was at the park to see the tricks of some jugglers from Valencia who had hired her as a representative of the people to decide on the program for their upcoming performance in the gardens of the Villa Medici. It was a date without a precise reason, the new thing was meeting up out in the open, just to see each other. But where, I wonder, did she meet these Spanish jugglers?

"At this point I've made the commitment, and so I have to go back to them shortly," she said to excuse herself after ten minutes, at the end of a granita di caffè.

I was looking around, surprised that I had never been inside this park. At the center was the avenue of the Domus Aurea, shaded by pine trees and big Lebanese cedars with the Colosseum in the background.

"I'm happy I came here. I wasn't familiar with this entrance to the Parco di Traiano, here at the top of Oppian Hill. I only knew the one below, on Via Labicana, closer to the Domus Aurea. Your jugglers picked a fantastic place."

I was happy to see Valeria in public without the furtive aura that adds atmosphere to the encounters of two secret lovers for a while, but in the long run becomes a torture. We were certainly two secret lovers, I said to myself, and even though I don't like this definition, not even a bit, I don't see what else we can be called — better not to be named at all, since we're a secret.

After about ten minutes, a glance at the empty glass of granita, and Valeria got up.

"I'm sorry, but now I have to go back to my Spanish friends."

I also got up, without showing the least disappointment. I was calm.

"Did you drive?"

Valeria walked with me to my car, parked next to the park entrance. A big statement stood out blatantly on the low wall next to a closed gate: "DIGOS³ murderer" and then a swastika. For some time now my eyes have run over the walls as if over an open book.

"Do you know that the villa hidden among the trees is the DIGOS headquarters?"

"Oh wow, what luxury."

I looked at the statement again, and I realized that the swastika was drawn backwards, with the legs counter-clockwise where they should have been turning towards the right, clockwise. It had a very strange effect that didn't remove the symbol's shame, but that mistake introduced an added sense of unease.

"How strange. The swastika's legs are drawn in reverse."

"I also thought there was something strange, but I couldn't figure out what."

"Can you imagine a dumbass drawing a swastika who is so dumb he gets it wrong?"

"Perhaps he's just left-handed."

"He's dumb anyway, left-handed and dumb. Or maybe he's being ironic. But I find it difficult to believe that someone who draws a swastika manages to be ironic by inverting the direction of the legs. Moreover, why do they hate the DIGOS so much that they draw a swastika right here? The DIGOS recently found the murderers of D'Antona and Biagi. I don't think the DIGOS deserves to be dumped in the trash."

"In the neighborhood they don't hate the DIGOS. They're jealous because they took the most beautiful villa in the area as their headquarters, half of which is inside the Parco di Traiano. That's what they told me at the café. And along the sidewalk they have reserved parking for twelve cars. And on top of that they even have a garage. What, do they want to throw parties?"

"A swastika. What do Nazis have to do with it? Today I'd defend the DIGOS from such an aggressive statement."

"Keep in mind that a little further up, on the other side of the park, there's the Caritas charity shop where a lot of illegal immigrants loiter. They might have some reasons to hate the DIGOS. The swastika is good for all the most idiotic uses."

A breeze with the strange and pleasant smell of vinegar ruffled the tree branches while buses were running on Via Labicana and the sirens of ambulances heading toward San Giovanni Hospital resounded in the air.

Valeria said goodbye in a hurry and rushed towards the avenue of the park to reach her juggler friends.

This is the miracle of topography: right there in front of the marvelous park of the Domus Aurea, with a view of the Colosseum, I had an indifferent encounter, with the only goal being to see Valeria *en plein air* for half an hour.

Nero's ghost was fluttering around there, followed by seagulls and crows.

I'm not used to snooping around Giano's papers. First of all because I wouldn't want to find out something unpleasant, and also out of respect for myself. However, this morning I found a piece of paper in plain view on his table. It had a statement written in small capital letters, "DIGOS murderers," and then a swastika. Where did he read this? What places does Giano visit without my knowledge? I already know that Giano stops to read the statements written on the walls, and sometimes he talks to me about them, but I didn't know he was jotting anything down. What's he going to do with them? Perhaps he writes them in his novel, an extra topic, a surprise for the reader. If he begins the book with the little story of the double-headed eagle, he can also add in the statements he reads on the walls.

For a few weeks now Giano's been carrying a notebook with him along with a black Pilot pen that he uses to write and draw (sketches and notes, not real drawings). And in the evenings he no longer indulges in the offerings on television. Instead, he huddles up on a couch and writes for a while, and then he starts reading *Don Quixote*, the only thing he's been reading for the last few months. And every once in a while he interrupts his reading and takes notes in his notebook. At a certain point he falls asleep with the book open on his lap.

A few evenings ago, when I went to wake him up on the couch, I read in his notebook a small title in capital letters, "The Death of a Friend." What friend? It was immediately clear that it was about Zandel. Zandel was the protagonist of those pages, or rather his death was. I don't understand what this piece of writing is good for. I think Giano is preparing a funeral eulogy, because the students and journalists will turn to him on that sad occasion.

Over the following days I realized that the pages on Zandel's death were visibly increasing. To judge from the thickness of the notebook, there were already more than about fifty of them. It couldn't have been a funeral eulogy, and not even an article to be published in an urban-planning journal, which wouldn't have been able to accommodate a text of that size. It was therefore a chapter of his novel, for I can't imagine Giano writing so many pages as a personal outpouring, or, we could even say, as a planned-out *post mortem* revenge.

Giano left his notebook on the table. It was almost an invitation for me to read it, and at the same time almost a joke on account of his handwriting, which was even worse than usual, basically cryptographic. I would like to know the purpose of such illegible handwriting, but it could also be a gratuitous game, one of his childish oddities just like telling little stories and paradoxes.

In the last few days, Giano has been leading our discussions strangely towards Zandel. I go along, and by talking about him I try to get rid of an intermittent nightmare that has been oppressing me for the last few months. It remerges at the most inappropriate moments. A great deal of talking about everything, about his vocation for lies, his ridiculous sidewalk urban planning that made him so much money, and how he and Irina have always managed to hide their wealth, to make it invisible. Shares, foreign bonds, most of all from Eastern European countries speculating on their admission into the European Union, but even these were only rumors generated by Zandel's frequent trips to Prague, Budapest, Warsaw. Financial speculations or sidewalk projects? Perhaps both, until the moment of the trip to New York, which marked the dividing line beyond which Zandel had become first absent, then ill, and in the end stabilized into the condition of a dying person.

Zandel was by that point a topic of conversation between the two of us. Perhaps Giano was simply looking for documentation for his writing. And sometimes he still tried to involve me in the nudist colony in Corsica. I was amazed by this insistence, which was inappropriate and by that point untimely. Perhaps he was hoping I'd fall into some contradiction, just like when they interrogate an alleged murderer and repeat the same questions a hundred times.

"Who knows how many times Zandel got laid in Corsica in the nudist village. I'm jealous of him, even if he only has one lung."

Sometimes Giano lets out statements as heavy as a rock, and most of the time I gloss over them for want of peace.

"I also thought that in those nudists' clubs that's all you do, but we learned from Zandel that it's not like that. People fuck the same as during the year in the city or in the countryside, in the summer or in the winter."

"It's a little different because you go there on vacation."

"Keep in mind that fucking, especially when it's hot, is tiring and a waste of energy."

"Fucking is the greatest form of enjoyment in the world. Climbing mountains is also tiring, and yet many wretches enjoy it so much."

"Fucking is not a sport."

"You can fuck for love, and you can even fuck for sport. I didn't get whether Zandel fucked that beautiful young woman from the pool, but I think so. Who knows whether it was for love or for sport."

Now Giano had arrived at the heart of the matter, and I was, you know, embarrassed, even though I was forcing myself to hide it.

"He was talking about it like a great, sentimental love."

"Sentimentality does not exclude fucking, quite the opposite."

"Considering how Zandel is doing, I fear we'll never satisfy this curiosity."

"The fact remains that they met at the nudist village."

"So what? I don't think it's enough."

"Think about it, a man meets a young woman among the nudists and decides to court her, both naked. Do you think it's like him meeting her in Rome on Via della Croce?"

"It's different," I had to admit.

Even now that his friend is surviving by force of transfusions and is no longer a competitor, Giano goes digging up his old jealousy aggravated that day by Zandel's resounding declaration for the young woman from the pool who had burned his heart. I still wonder whether, in his subconscious, Giano had identified her, that young woman, and had understood that it was Clarissa. These interrogations make me lean towards a yes, but, on the other hand, they could just be the obsessive voice of jealousy.

In memory of Zandel's resounding declaration of love, I ate another chocolate.

GIANO

I'm sure Clarissa managed to read I don't know how many pages of my book — I don't dare call it a novel yet. Perhaps her interest in a story where she is the protagonist has distracted and deflected her from the idea of having a conversation about Valeria, as she had threatened. Perhaps I've avoided embarrassment and danger.

One of the main characters of the book is ambiguous, fleeting and even a bit ridiculous, because he made his fortune as an urban planner by designing the sidewalks of big European cities. He's a character that fits very well inside a modern novel, even though an illness has isolated him from the world. If this same urban planner is then fixated on naked women, that voyeuristic tendency emphasizes his ambiguity and generates some suspicion about his qualities as a lover.

Zandel has never hidden that he didn't pass up the chance to visit art galleries and museums whenever he went on business trips, most of all to collect images of naked women. He always used to make a distinction about artistic nudes, which above all spurred snickers among his students. An interview published in the journal, *Belfagor*, also gave rise to the bitter laughter of academic critics. In a language that parodied the rigid rhetoric of the university, Zandel appropriated the theory of an eccentric art critic who divided paintings of nudes into "single-ass" and "double-ass," depending on the point of view assumed by the painter. During that long interview Zandel patiently listed and commented on the drawings and paintings he had seen and recorded from museums around the world and from frescos viewed in palaces and castles. At times he commented with a simple adjective and other times with brief personal impressions.

The first row of the single-asses included Eve and Adam in the Sistine Chapel's fresco of the Original Sin. Adam was one of the few men admitted to his collection. Part of the same category were an exciting Leda — once again by Michelangelo — the kneeling female single-ass by Raphael, a romantic single-ass by Ingres, an odalisque and the woman with parrot by Delacroix, an odalisque by Corot, an imperial single-ass by Velázquez, the pen drawing of a Venus who's holding the apple received from Paris by Hans Baldung Grien, and, in more recent paintings, a female single-ass by Gromaire, one by Munch, and one by Klee, early style.

The double-ass category was more crowded, beginning with the marvelous central subject of the Three Graces in the Villa of the Mysteries in Pompei; a tremendous double-ass in pen in the foreground among Albrecht Dürer's bathers; the lady at the center among the Three Graces by Raphael; two elegant double-asses by Ingres; three wonderful, moving double-asses by Pisanello, drawn by pen on parchment; an elegant double-ass of Venus at the mirror by Velázquez; the smooth Graces by Antonio Canova. But the list also included an overweight double-ass by Tintoretto, an Angelica by Titian, the left of two witches by Hans Baldung Grien, and more double-asses by Rembradt, Renoir, Watteau, Fragonard, Delacroix, Degas, Gauguin and Casorati.

In the interview for *Belfagor*, next to the information on each painting, Zandel had jotted down the date, the museum or place where he had seen it, and most of the time he also mentioned the title of the art books or magazines where reproductions of the paintings were located, synthetically listed in two categories: Sgl. and Dbl. "List totally incomplete," Zandel had noted at the end of the interview.

My thought: the two categories could have only been applied to the static figures in painting and sculpture because the young woman from the nudist village in Corsica moved her ass in all directions, and it could be seen from both points of view.

Through his book Giano represents me with love and resentment, but he's always close to the truth or, in any case, to a possible or probable image of reality. His intuitions and his hypotheses end up unveiling my feelings and my sins through Marozia and sometimes they even give me suggestions. I read anything that concerns my persona with attention, even when it takes a wrong turn. For instance, the crisis of loneliness that spurred me to go to Barcelona — the idea that the driving force was loneliness was a serious blunder. His disappointment after an evening and a night spent with that big-ass Valeria was a surprise.

A few lines further down, a dogmatic statement hit me like a slap across the face. It surprised and offended me. "The truth," Giano writes, "is that Marozia is a bit of a whore." So, Giano thinks that I, too, am a bit of a whore, since I am the model for Marozia. Why a bit? One is either a whore or not. And two lines further on, suddenly, there's a quote from the Bible: "Next time, the fire." Is that a threat? Directed at whom? A little higher up, I am the subject, so is it directed at me? Do I have to be afraid for my life? You never know. Giano is having fun scattering suspicions and threats. Perhaps he has suspicions about Luccio? Or perhaps something more than a suspicion? I wouldn't want to lose my health over a few excesses. I'm worried.

I'd like to go on reading even though this horrible handwriting is poking my eyes and the words upset me, but I have a date at Luccio's office at four o'clock, and I can't miss these opportunities to satisfy my orphaned feelings and my exuberant hormones.

Outside it's pouring, and I try to call a cab on my cell phone even though Luccio's office is very close. Naturally, when it rains it's hard to find a cab that's available in Rome, so I decided to walk in the rain with my umbrella. In any case, I will arrive in Via della Stelletta in wet clothes, and I want to see if Luccio will want to make love without undressing me. He's absolutely capable of it.

I'm not sure whether I should tell him Zandel's idea about the single-asses and double-asses, and I didn't tell him that I'm secretly reading Giano's novel where I am the protagonist. I still want to think about it before revealing such secrets.

And Dulcinea, what does Dulcinea say?

GIANO

I am now positive that Clarissa secretly reads a few pages of my book every day. She's been very anxious recently, and she takes a Xanax pill every morning — I've counted the pills in the box, there's nothing wrong with that. There is no trace of this reading in any of her behavior. It's true that her reading must certainly be full of gaps on account of my handwriting, but even reduced in that way, the text can't leave her indifferent. Either she's a monster of self-control or else at a certain point she will burst, and I'm waiting for her reaction to create a turning point in my novel. It is the novel itself that will provoke the next narrative turning points, through Clarissa's secret reading and her reactions, which I keep under control. On the one hand, her behavior will be influenced by my pages. Let's watch this. On the other, these pages will unfold bearing Clarissa's behavior in mind.

In the end, I've realized that writing a novel inspired by characters who are living acquaintances is a real mess of identity. I'm a bit disoriented, but I'm happy to be breathing, and I won't give up.

"I'd like to find an opportunity to introduce you to my husband," I told Luccio. "A friendly relationship would make our encounters easier, and they could extend beyond the horizon of your couch."

Luccio remained silent for a while, perhaps offended by the irony about his couch.

"It won't be easy. We have different interests."

"Ultimately, urban planning like my husband's, which applies to the City of the Future, could have a place in your studies on social life in modern cities."

"Why not? Your husband on the future of the city, Lucci Nerissi on the future of urban society."

"Let's wait for the right occasion."

Every time I do even the smallest project with Luccio, my thoughts run toward Zandel, who is condemned to inertia and suffering not only in reality, but even in the novel that Giano is writing. By now Zandel is cut off from everything and everyone. He wishes to be forgotten, I have to assume, condemned to a *damnatio memoriae* that he himself wanted, and this really amazes me.

What kind of existence is his? Is it worth living in those conditions? Who knows why I happen to think about poor Johannes, who died at night on the road to Frankfurt with a terrible crash of metal sheets. Which fate is worse? But I realize this is a useless thought, one to be immediately forgotten.

I'm offended, and the box of chocolates is not enough to diminish the offense. If I decide to dedicate a thought to you with a chocolate, I communicate to you simply that with your silence you are throwing me, you have thrown me, into Luccio's arms. I would have preferred a brief phone call instead of your sixty chocolates. Among other things, I have to watch my figure because half an ounce of chocolate is enough to make me gain a couple of pounds, contrary to all the laws of physics. Or is wanting to make me gain weight one of your many fantasies?

As you can see, I've become suspicious of everybody at every opportunity.

GIANO

It was during a public discussion in the city council on variations to the plan for the Sant'Egidio neighborhood, north of the Tiburtina Station, that, talking with the council member for the suburbs, a beautiful blonde woman who was very slim, I proposed a secondary application of my Urban Deconstruction. Finally people understand that many urban planning operations now have to start with the demolition of structures that are out of place and, obviously, obsolete ones. In New York, up until a few decades ago, when a skyscraper got old it was torn down and replaced by a new one, with the exception of the few skyscrapers elevated to the status of symbols, such as the Empire State Building or the vanished, defunct Twin Towers.

One of the city architects observed that, in any case, this is a luxury that perhaps only a rich city like Chicago can afford. Thank you, thank you for the update. But then, as usual, I received many theoretical approvals and tight-lipped acknowledgements of my urban-planning categories.

When the meeting ended, Clarissa, who was in the audience, introduced me to that fellow, Lucci Nerissi, whom she had met at Castel Sant'Angelo during the party for Einaudi — the one she saw again in Barcelona together with her friend whom she met at the salon. This guy, Lucci Nerissi, has the quite unpleasant look of a Turk from Anatolia, like those men who appear in Muslim iconography: dark skin, black moustache and a low forehead. I had to agree to Clarissa's request to make a stop at the café at the corner of Piazza Campitelli, but I didn't want to sit down with that Turcoman. I don't like him, but I noticed that he and Clarissa are very informal and, therefore, I had to be informal too. But, I repeat, I don't like him. At a certain point, I came down with a fit of allergic coughing. I seemed to be on the verge of spitting out my lungs. This doesn't mean anything, I said to myself, but someone like that, I don't want to see him ever again. In the end, he understood that I didn't have the slightest affection for him, and finally we said goodbye very coldly.

"But where the hell does this strange character come from?"

"Why strange?"

"He looks like a genetically modified product."

"I met him during the party at Castel Sant'Angelo, where you were as well, and then, together with my friend, I saw him again by chance in Barcelona at a café on the Rambla de Santa Mònica.

That's it. Then I found him again here, today, in the audience during your polemic on the Tiburtina Variation."

"By chance, did you invite him to this meeting?"

"No, why?"

"Just asking."

I can't understand how my wife can be friendly with such a callous and physically unpleasant person. At a certain point I heard that she was calling him Luccio, and I remembered that during her agitated sleep Clarissa begged for Luccio's help more than once. I couldn't figure out what was happening to her because in dreams there are no capitalized letters, and in lowercase letters *luccio* is just a fresh water fish. That said, I refuse to be jealous of such a callous fellow who, among other things, sneezes like a hippopotamus. Naturally I've decided he will never set foot in my novel because of his obvious unworthiness, but this is not the problem. The problem is Clarissa.

Clarissa takes advantage of her hours of loneliness when I'm in Valle Giulia to read a few more pages of my novel. With much effort she'll manage to decipher my horrible handwriting, and she'll be surprised because in the events filtered through my imagination, it's possible to recognize secret facts, of which we two are or were the protagonists. For instance, a possible relationship of hers with Zandel before his illness — which in the novel becomes a certainty — and a possible relationship of mine with Valeria — which in the novel becomes another certainty. I don't want to investigate any further so as not to run into new, more unpleasant and painful certainties. No, no, I'm not talking about the heart. The heart hasn't got shit to do with it.

In case I decide to publish it, and if I find a publisher, naturally at the beginning of the book I will insert the usual epitaph to explain that the characters and the events in which they are involved are exclusively the fruit of my imagination, and they do not refer to persons or facts from so-called reality. Although, to ward off any suspicions, it would be better to state that the facts and characters are inspired by facts and characters from real life. A statement like that would push readers to think the exact opposite because a writer, everyone knows, is a liar by vocation. If within herself Clarissa recognizes the truth of the stories I write about her — as Marozia, obviously — I already know she will never admit it, and she will profusely compliment me for my lively imagination.

In the meantime I'm still waiting for Clarissa to react to her reading, to show some sign of her clandestine encounter with my book.

Giano and Luccio didn't like each other. Too bad, but I'm not going to pull my hair out over it. I should have been able to foresee it, but instead I naively believed they could find a glimmer of communication together. The result: a little worse than nothing.

I struggled to read a few more pages of Giano's book, and I found confirmation of a fact I had suspected, namely that he really intends to publish this so-called novel of his. It has become fashionable, or rather a mania: politicians, singers, entrepreneurs, serious academics, television hosts, the unemployed, illustrious hookers, slackers, everyone has written or intends to write a novel. Why? Novels talk about everything, adventures improvisations games of life dramas paradoxes descriptions imaginations philosophies psychologies stories about sex and melancholy violence feelings and intelligence. For this reason, everybody likes novels, both to read and to write. There, everything concentrates or vaporizes, according to the skills the talent the creativity the language and the intentions of the author. Even a successful urban planner like Giano already has his novel almost good to go, and you'll see, dear Clarissa, he will find a publisher and, why not, he's even capable of winning a literary award.

It's true though that a publication and even an award are not enough to make a writer out of an urban planner. But this is Giano's ambition, because the book is constructed in two voices, following the technique of "exterior monologue." This was already employed a few years ago by an Italian writer who successfully rewrote the encounter between Penelope and Ulysses after the Homeric hero's return to Ithaca. In that case, it was a love duel between the two protagonists, Ulysses and Penelope, while this book uncovers the inglorious betrayals of two professionals and their respective wives and lovers. Giano continues writing without amazement and without regret, hopping like a tarantula. And, just like the insect, he carries a dose of painful but not lethal poison.

A bit of eroticism, fine, but the way Giano describes my encounters with Zandel is absolutely fantastic and precisely for this reason — I have to proudly confess — quite close to reality. I hadn't imagined that Giano could have such vibrant creativity in the erotic field, and I don't understand why for quite some time he hasn't performed his personal Kamasutra in bed with me. Our bed is now arid, Giano would say, like the sands of the Sahara.

In this novel Giano mixes a big concoction of experiences and inventions, which he makes plausible by copying people from real life but with different names. What made me mad is obviously not the morbid eroticism attributed to me and Zandel — which is to say Marozia and Zurlo — but that secret encounter in Strasbourg with Tania (Valeria), his gift of cyclamens to that whore as if she were a noble lady. In reality Valeria is a real slut, always ready to couple with anyone on her radar: a fuck and move on. If Giano is happy with that, good for him, but ever since he spent a night at her place, it seems like his opinion of her has plummeted. The only thing that surprises me is that it took him so long to figure it out.

It's hard for me to include in my book, as I would like to, a series of graffiti that could give meaning to the wandering impulses that move on the city walls. Sometimes a generically anarchic inspiration emerges from these statements. But they always make one perceive the dismay of the youth, their despair and rage against everything and everyone that makes the heart freeze up. These graffiti are just the volatile symptom in spray of who knows how many hidden and explosive energies. But also how much confusion is diffused by this urban paint, if we want to welcome the daring synthesis "Sex Mix," proposed in purple-red paint on a wall of Piazza Euclide — which is part of a neighborhood marked off in green in my demolition project. Should I perhaps propose a shred of interpretation of the graffiti phenomenon? Actually no. Perhaps it's fairer to leave the statements alone, just as they are, and each time to delegate the onus of mural hermeneutics to readers of a postmodern vocation. For instance, it's difficult to reconcile messages on ethics and banks with the announcement in big letters "God exists," which in reality doesn't indicate the presence of God but that of heroin.

Another issue. As for the framework of my book, what do I do with Zandel? I've arrived at page 147, and for about one hundred of them, namely, since his return from New York, Zandel has always been irremediably sick, perhaps dying. One cannot abuse the patience of the reader, who has been expecting his death since he stopped appearing as a character and only as a sick person. I have to address this problem, especially when I find an editor willing to publish me. However, I feel that killing Zandel point-blank this far into the book, even if his name is Zurlo, is a criminal action to the detriment of a friend. Even if our friendship has expired little by little — I almost wrote exsanguinated — since Zandel got sick and started refusing to see his friends. I don't dislike a character who is ashamed of being sick, but I don't know to what extent readers will like him.

Meanwhile in reality I feel so bad for poor Zandel, and I regret the outings in his company when he used to court Clarissa, spurring my jealousy but also a subtle erotico-social excitement. Unfortunately as a character he is really misbehaving, and I just don't know what decision to make.

There are so many problems and so much stress in writing a novel. I have to thank God that I am an urban planner and nobody is forcing me to be a writer. However, since I have already jotted down so many pages, it's better for me to keep going because in the end I've found out, I must admit, that I have fun writing even if fatigue and stress are included in the fun.

CLARISSA

I don't know how to explain it. The trip to Barcelona made me realize that I'm not happy with Luccio, but I didn't quite understand what wasn't right with him. We perform long corvées in bed, in all directions. It's an ongoing transgression, especially since I convinced him to make love naked. (With Luccio I've discovered my vocation for the most licentious kinds of eroticism, the discovery that every hole of the body is a place of pleasure.) But it's not enough for me. The magic is missing, the hermetic grain of words — his beautiful voice is no longer enough — the warmth that enwraps, that fills up the space around us, in other words, that fortunate relaxation that is indispensable for a relationship of love.

We will never see the rainbow together.

It's actually true: Luccio is callous and laconic. During the trip to Barcelona he barely spoke to me on the plane, and when he says something, the words seem to be said to be forgotten. I hadn't realized it, but ever since Giano pointed out how he looks like a Turk from Anatolia, he has become unbearable to me. It's more than enough of a reason to break off this relationship with such a brutally laconic man, who has a low forehead and hair as black as tar and as coarse as horsehair and who — Giano is right — sneezes like a hippopotamus. Unfortunately Giano has been absent in bed for quite some time now, but I will live without him just like I will live without Luccio.

Who knows, perhaps I also have to weigh in the balance that I'm sorry for betraying Zandel, who is sick. I haven't seen him for four months now, but while he is still alive, every time I meet up with Luccio I feel like I'm betraying both Zandel and Giano together. I suddenly have a desperate desire to see the rainbow in the company of Zandel, hugging each other tightly, a few words and long kisses. I'm consumed by my thoughts. And him, if only he were so nice as to give me a call for once.

It's a painful situation, almost unbearable, this presence — this absence — of Zandel, who is exaggeratedly sick. I don't mean by this that it would be better if he died. I'd be a monster if I had such a thought — I did have it, unfortunately. However, as long as he is alive and so sick, I feel a great compassion towards him, and I often see his eyes watching me right when I make love with Luccio, and I say to myself, you are a slut, a goddamn slut. This thought is worth at least two chocolates upon my return home.

On the other hand, Zandel is becoming a problem even for his friends. Giano, for example, after the unpleasant and obsessive memories of the nudists, now does everything in his power not to mention him. I think that he, too, is embarrassed by his friend's presence–absence, but it would be more correct to say ex-friend. What kind of friendship can exist with a dying person who refuses to see the people who love him?

I'm travelling like a vagabond amidst Giano's pages, and I've started to decipher the text where he once again talks about the nudist colony in Corsica. Now what we need to understand is whether my presence among the nudists is the result of Giano's morbid and obsessive imagination, or if he really understood how things went. I will never get out of this muddle between fiction and reality. It still surprises me how more than once in this book the novelistic imagination draws dangerously close to the truth. And vice versa — no matter the situation, saying vice versa always works. And in the meantime Giano's obsession has now become my obsession. And vice versa.

Everybody knows that many writers get the inspiration for their novels from real people. In this way fictional characters happen to have a longer life than their flesh-and-blood models. How long ago did the people disappear who were human models for novels and stories by, for instance, Thomas Mann or Italo Svevo? Meanwhile, their respective written characters are always there, on the page, in excellent health. I don't know how long Giano's novel will last, but if it is published certainly the printed page will last longer than Zandel —big deal — but perhaps also longer than we who have normal life expectancies.

Poor Zandel and poor us, who have neither a Thomas Mann nor an Italo Svevo who can comfortably and enduringly establish us inside some nice book. And don't think now that I despise my husband because he's not Thomas Mann or Italo Svevo.

GIANO

Well, I had almost decided to conclude my novel with Zurlo's death, but I've realized I can't run the risk that a death invented in the novel happens in conjunction with the real death of poor Zandel. Who would be able to undo my reputation as being a jinx? I'm not the only one who is superstitious. The world is full of superstitious people. And thus I'll only be able to write about Zurlo's death after Zandel's death. But can I predicate the death of a character in my novel on that of his flesh-and-blood model? I ought to sit here and wait, risking that at a certain point I will lose my patience and wish for my friend's death. I already caught myself more than once, ashamed, thinking how wonderful if he died. Isn't that already too much?

Anyway, it's an embarrassing situation. In the worst case, I can leave the matter on hold and end the book with a Zurlo who is sick and goes on being sick. But can you end a novel leaving the life of one of the protagonists on hold? Undoubtedly the character's death would be a more satisfying ending for the readers, especially if one takes into consideration all the crap he did to the detriment of Bubi throughout the whole book.

CLARISSA

I went on with my reading, if my struggle to decipher this text can be called reading, with a few words here and there that I can't understand and, as for the rest, I try to guess. I keep being astonished: Giano perceived my secret relationship with Zandel in all of its special moments as if he had observed us through the keyhole. He's only wrong in his description of the setting where we used to see each other, a *garçonnière* in the art-deco style, just like, I believe, were once used for kept whores. When he wants to play writer, poor Giano, he lags a century behind.

Giano and I will never be able to know to what extent our betrayals are reciprocal, because on this topic there is no dialogue between us (I don't want to mention Luccio). We've gone on for twenty years with our compact — residential tolerance — and after such a long time we obviously can't sit ourselves down to engage in self-criticism and blurt out everything to each other's face, like certain friends of our generation who all ended up very badly with nervous breakdowns and lawyers. Giano and I are pointed out as a model of marital success, and we can't disappoint the world.

As far as I'm concerned, I decided to leave Luccio as long as Zandel is alive (three chocolates), but mostly because Giano is right about him: he looks like a horrible Turcoman from Anatolia. I don't know yet with what excuse I'll be able to justify my departure. Obviously I won't be able to tell him the truth: look, an ex-lover of mine is very sick and as long as he is alive I must be faithful to him because we never broke up, it was just his illness that kept us apart. In other words, the situation is still on hold. That Luccio wears me out with boredom, I can only think in silence. I certainly won't tell that to him or to anyone else. I can't even reveal to him that I'm breaking up with him because of a word: I can no longer have anything to do with a Turcoman — moreover a terribly laconic one — much less sleep with him. And I also want to erase the memory of him. But I'm sure it will erase itself.

It happens that an absent and sick Zandel still influences my life and indirectly even that of Bubi — every time I mention Bubi I hear the usual dog that barks in my ears, poor Giano. I'm sorry that I have to wait for the death of such a loving person as Zandel in order to finally be free in my behavior as a human. A "finally" escaped me, and this could make you think that I can't wait for him to die, poor Zandel. I'm a slut, but not to that extreme.

I ate four chocolates one after the other on account of four nice thoughts making up for one bad thought. But I'm tired of obeying Zandel like a mole while he, sick as he is, could at least give me a call, right?

GIANO

I would like to be able to write like Cervantes, but I won't even try, since I already know that I will never be able to do it. I can declare my dismay, but I could also decide to burn the notebooks with everything in them. Perhaps I would have been better off if I had stuck with those two initials I wrote on the cover and had written a book about my Urban Deconstruction, a topic that I know well, instead of venturing into the thorny thicket of truth and fiction. These are entangled in our bourgeois world, but perhaps also in all societies of all times, because associating truth and fiction is typical of humans. But there's a terrible word written among the others in my book, and just like the merchant who received the certainty of Christ's miracle from his wife, I will know with glaring certainty when Clarissa has read it, because it will be impossible to avoid a reaction from her like the reaction to an electric shock.

CLARISSA

I haven't seen Luccio again, and I don't even want to see him. I thought about visiting the pharmacist's wife, but I feel ashamed about telling her how I fell into such a vulgar story. And I don't even know whether it's a story at all. Perhaps it's better for me to go tell her my medical issue, my dizziness and the knot in my stomach. Perhaps she can give me something that will help me stand on my feet, because all the Xanax does is to make me catatonic and drowsy for the entire day. According to him, according to Xanax, I have to accept this passing state of mine and not care about the confusion produced in my head. This, too, shall pass.

I don't want to see Luccio again. Making love on that couch where who knows how many women have been, I've had enough. I don't even know how it all started. It must have been a moment of weakness, or loneliness, as Valeria says to justify her fucks on the go. In any case, I said enough, I no longer want to see that boor with his Turcoman face. Let him go find someone else for his afternoon fucks, or rather go to Tor di Quinto or on the Salaria, where he can find women in plenty who are suitable for him.

Luccio called my cell phone for the fourth time. I set up a date with him, and for the fourth time I stood him up. I believe he understood, because he never called again. But now what do I do with my mortal life, all alone with Giano who is as inert as sawdust?

And Dulcinea, what does Dulcinea say?

I don't understand where this nice box of Swiss chocolates came from. Clarissa hid it in the closet underneath the woolen scarfs. Zandel would be capable of giving her chocolates, but I don't really think he's in the mood for such a frivolous, worldly gesture. Who else then? That clodhopper, Lucci Nerissi, who Clarissa claims to have run into again by chance — by chance, exclamation mark — in Barcelona? I might be wrong, but it's not his type of gesture.

Chocolates can replace flowers as a thank you for an invitation or as a move to come closer for the conquest of a lady. But they don't belong, I'm sure, to the language of that Turcoman. It could be a new suitor of Clarissa's, then, since Zandel is no longer in the running and Lucci Nerissi is not the chocolate type. I will eat about ten chocolates, so that Clarissa will know I've discovered her secret. But I hope she won't say anything because I would never want to waste five minutes talking about chocolates, which have already occupied my thoughts for too long. Everyone knows that thinking confuses ideas, but thinking about the source of these chocolates is like proposing to scientifically analyze a question mark drawn by Clarissa, who is a champion at reticence.

To exorcise the event, I will give Clarissa a box of Perugina Baci, so she will be able to read the little notes inside containing sayings of chocolatière wisdom. I remain on the side of Cervantes and his generous Hidalgo.

Clarissa will certainly realize that some chocolates are missing and that only I could have taken them — the maid is out of the question. If she wants, she will talk to me about it. Otherwise, even this obscure and frivolous message will end up like so many other discussions left incomplete and stored in the dense wire fence that enwraps our lives. Assuming that behind every message — words or chocolates — there is a shred of truth, in the end I don't give a damn about this truth.

I say something, and immediately after I regret having said it. I, too, have my moments of despair, and every now and then I hide in the bathroom to cry with no tears and no words. I borrow the words from an old Italian poet, with a faded cover that I opened by chance while I was organizing my library. The poet shares his despair with the whole world, and he sees the stars, the moon and the nocturnal air cry over his lover's death.

What dew or what weeping,
what tears were those
I saw bestrewn from the dark veil of night
and from the white, dazzling face of the stars?
And why did the white moon scatter
a pure cloud of crystalline drops
on the lap of cool grass?
Why in the dark air
was there heard, almost grieving, the breezes
wandering all around till day-break?
Were these perhaps signs of your departure,
life of my life?[4]

Poor Torquato, he must have suffered very much. But the stars were crying and the white moon was crying for him, whereas nobody cries for me. It's true that Clarissa is not dead, but inside me, she is now more than dead, after her story with that despicable Turcoman. And I let it all out with a few solitary laments, and then I take off again on my improvised navigation by sight, life of my life.

Seven chocolates are missing from the box, perhaps a few more. I interrogated the maid with great discretion. She didn't even know I had hidden the chocolate box in the closet. So it's Giano, then. It was Giano. I'm not sure. I don't know how to talk about it. What to tell him. There's always the solution we've adopted every time to resolve our embarrassments: pretend nothing happened.

Last night I had two very strange dreams, perhaps interesting, and I wanted to tell Giano.

The first dream. I can't define the environment we are in. A student, whom I've never seen but who is certainly Giano's student, shows up in front of me. The student is holding a heavy marble bust, which portrays a character with a moustache and a low forehead. He asks me to introduce him to Federico Zeri. Mind that I barely knew the great critic, who had passed away, however, I knew where to find him. I take the student to a small museum in Corso Vittorio Emanuele where, in fact, we find Zeri, who greets the student coldly, examines the marble bust without uttering a word, then reaches with his arms and hefts it up. After a few instants he drops the bust to the ground, and it shatters. It's not clear whether Zeri dropped it on purpose, which is possible considering his mischievous personality, or whether the heavy bust fell accidentally. The student starts crying desperately, and I flee. End of the first dream. I've forgotten the second.

I told Giano about this dream with a famous character like Zeri inside it, to see whether he will insert it in his book. In other words, I would prefer to not always be passive with regard to Giano's novel, but to suggest some topics of my own. I always hope that, especially if stimulated by some new topic, Giano will take my ideas into account and that he doesn't just consider me from a sexual point of view, which, by the way, is a habit that's been missing between us for a few months now. Right at the moment I got rid of Luccio, and abstinence is not my forte.

I miss Zandel, and now I also miss that beast, Luccio. But I did well to leave him because Giano is right when he says he's a callous man. Therefore, I say, he's not worthy of being my lover.

Oh my God, my God. I went back to read some lines about Luccio, which I had skipped over because of the difficult handwriting. In two lines, which were as dry as a rifle shot, Giano says that Lucci Nerissi is notoriously HIV p. This is my death, announced in a few words by Giano. So life, already brief like a puff of wind, will be taken away from me by an illness, which will carry me off in sorrow and shame.

I didn't think about using a condom. I never imagined that a man of his age could carry that damned illness. HIV p., Giano writes, but unfortunately there is no doubt about the meaning of the word: I recognize Giano's hypocrisy. For instance, he would never write the word cancer, which seems obscene to him. I recognize it. Even when he talks about sex he says bush and grapes, to avoid saying pussy and cock. Musing about it is useless. Luccio is HIV positive, and consequently I, too, am HIV positive. Oh fuck.

Goddamned Luccio, I hope you die soon, and damn those obscene fucks on the couch like two gypsies. I don't know where Giano got this news from, but certainly at the university, where voices carry, and everybody knows everything about everybody. For an instant I hoped it was a fictional invention of Giano's, but the whole novel is inspired by absolutely true facts, unfortunately, and therefore, even this horrible news is certainly true.

I immediately called a doctor from the national health center, and he told me that in order to know anything for sure I'd have to check it in six months because in any case there would be no results right now. And me, what am I going to do for these six months? What am I going to do? Shall I shoot myself? Whether it's positive or not, the doctor said he will give me the test results regardless, and only then will I have to decide what to do. He said regardless. How heavy words are in certain cases. This is his job, and for him it's the same thing whether the tests are positive or not. What does he care about my life?

Ambulance sirens resound on the streets of Rome. They run over my skin like pieces of ice. My hands are shaking, and my head is wrapped in the fumes of despair.

Now I understand why Giano has stopped making love to me for quite some time now, ever since I had the damned affair with that damned Turcoman. But then, if he knew that Luccio was HIV positive, why didn't he tell me? This is murder, I was murdered by Giano. He realized that I would sleep with Luccio ever since the day of that party at Castel Sant'Angelo, and he wanted to take his revenge. I'm sure that the Biblical threat "Next time, the fire" referred to my relationship with Luccio. But making me die over a few fucks is worse than those husbands who stab their wives to death. At least they are confronted with a trial and jail. He found a way to murder me free of charge, risk free. And I deserve it because I behaved like a whore. I allowed myself to be fucked on a couch right on the spur of the moment, with no condom with no thoughts with no love like the last whore of Tor di Quinto. Actually no, whores use condoms.

I already know what I will do when they give me the results: I'll go to Africa, to Mozambique, to treat people infected with AIDS. In any case I'm not afraid of infection since I'm already infected. Twenty-five million infected people in Africa. A continent that is drowning. I will go to Africa, to Mozambique, and I'll drown together with the African continent. Far away from Rome, far away from shame. But why wait for the results, which can only be positive? I'll sell the shares that Giano put in my name, and I'll leave immediately. I can't manage this fiction for six months. Everybody will think that I had a fit of rapture for Médecins Sans Frontières, which I'll join in Mozambique. This way I will at least save face if not my life.

Giano's book disappeared right at the moment that I'd like to read my death sentence again and go on reading that page to understand what else Giano wrote, and whether he realizes he sentenced me to death. Otherwise, what sense does it make writing in the book that Lucci Nerissi is HIV positive? I already knew that his book is a *cloaca* where all the bullshit of our bourgeois world finds its place, recounted with perverse taste. Despite all this, reading it had become a point of communication in Zandel's absence. I managed to give a meaning to what I was doing, whereas now I am a woman lost in the ocean with no compass to show me what direction to take. I feel the emptiness underneath my feet to the point that certain days I stay home without moving and don't even answer the phone. If I could at least talk to Zandel. But if I told him the truth, I would never have his forgiveness. I will go die in Africa along with the elephants.

Giano's book had become a parallel mirror where I saw myself sometimes as a friendly figure and other times as a person burdened with terrible faults. That damned, nibbled word was a sudden flash of lightning, and now I am a poor woman, defeated and vaporized, who no longer knows where to beat her ass. A whore like Valeria who fucked *urbis et orbis* is as healthy as a hare, and I am sentenced to die an atrocious death. The world's injustice is infinite. I have a high esteem for God, but then why did he betray me?

I looked everywhere, in the closets where clothes are, inside all the furniture including the dish cabinets, I even took the ladder and I looked high up on top of the closets. Nothing. It's clear that Giano's book is no longer to be found in our home. Did he perhaps take it to a print shop or to the university to have it typed on a computer by a student? That seems to be the most likely thing. But God forbid he burnt it or threw it out into the Tiber, because I need to know something more. I want to read those damned words again and understand what they reveal or what they hide. I can't ask Giano who told him that Luccio is HIV positive. It would be like confessing that I slept with him. Although Giano knows it, I don't want to confess it. Even I have my fucking dignity.

I would like to think that Giano made it all up in revenge when he figured out or suspected that I was sleeping with Luccio and found out I was reading his book. Unfortunately that's not what happened, because ever since I started seeing Luccio, Giano stopped making love to me. He knew I was infected. It's totally clear.

I'm trying to convince Clarissa to go see a neurologist because there is no doubt that she's had a major breakdown. I don't think Zandel's illness is the cause, even though it's one of the reasons for her depression. Her collapse happened a few days ago, and it certainly coincides with her reading the few lines where I relay the news that Lucci Nerissi is HIV positive. If she's so desperate, I have confirmation of what I already knew, in other words, that she had a sexual affair with him. Naturally, she said she doesn't need a doctor, as everyone with nervous illnesses says. In the meantime, she has nightmares all night, and more than once when I came home, I saw that her eyes were red from crying. It seems that crying is good for depressed people. Some doctors in antiquity used to prescribe crying as a treatment. (Hippocrates? Galen?)

In the garbage bin in the kitchen I found the box of chocolates that Clarissa had hidden in the closet. The cardboard box was smashed in anger, the chocolates scattered among potato skins and chicken bones. A further sign of her serious disturbances.

I'm afraid that soon I'll be depressed, too, when the copyist returns the text of my novel to me, all printed in gleaming Garamond. I will read it all at once. At the moment I don't consider it finished, but it's now so far along that I need to carefully read over everything that I wrote following the thread of my memory. If I consider it worthwhile, I'll go on writing, keeping my eyes wide open to everything that happens around me, the ongoing paradox of life. This is the reason why I'm afraid my novel will never end if I'm not able to give a conclusion to a character like Zandel, who has remained there between life and death for several months now.

Unfortunately I don't have the courage to make Zurlo-Zandel die, and I've been hauling him along like a ball and chain for too long now. Clarissa's despair could conclude my book in a dramatic way, but do I have the courage to exploit my wife's despair to write a few dramatic pages? My weak writing isn't capable of keeping up with such a desperate reality.

I lost all interest in Giano's funereal novel, and even if I were to find it right in front of my eyes, I won't ever again try to read those pages that include my death sentence. Giano did well to hide that notebook, which deserved nothing but fire or the waters of the Tiber. I live in despair and shame because I won't be able to keep my plight secret for much longer. What will I tell Giano? And what will I tell our friends? That I am HIV positive, or better HIV p. as Giano writes, since he is repulsed by certain words that are too painful or too shameful? It's better to leave right away. Africa is better.

According to the doctor at the national health center, it isn't a hundred per cent certain that I've been infected because life and human relationships are not like math, but I'm sure he's just saying that because he sensed my despair. It wasn't one but fifty, a hundred rough, deep fucks. And each time that damned Turcoman was injecting me with the deadly virus. And he knew it. Of course he knew it, but he, too, will drop dead. Of course he will. Those orgasms without happiness and love are now costing me so much despair.

To make me feel better, the doctor from the national health center said that there are many HIV-positive people even in Rome, many more than one would think, and that I'll be able to go on with my normal life, don't forget the condom. But now that I'm infected, what do I need the condom for? The doctor said: But don't you think about other people? I was ashamed.

Later on the nice doctor made me understand that he wouldn't mind sleeping with me in order to show me that my condition is acceptable, always using a condom, of course. I wish I were in the mood, but it's not really the time for these things, poor unhappy mammal. I feel as if my life is escaping me from every angle. How many years or how many months of life remain before me? HIV-positive people don't die right away. Sometimes they even live up to ten years, and in ten years they will certainly discover a cure. Actually no. I will beg death to arrive soon. May it arrive immediately to take me away from sorrow and shame. My last impossible wish: I would like to die together with Zandel. In the same bed.

I let Giano know that I intended to go to Africa to treat people infected with AIDS with the Médecins Sans Frontières. Giano didn't blink an eye, and in this way he confirmed what he wrote in the book. If it were just an invention of his, he certainly wouldn't let me leave.

I already bought the ticket for a flight to Mozambique, the capital of Mozambique.

"First ethics and then science." Is this perhaps the path I must follow ever since the moment I decided to write a novel? Ethics suggests that I respect Zandel's illness, whereas my narrative is telling me his life is only an obstacle and that, for this reason, there's nothing respectable about it.

Now Clarissa, too, has entered death row, and I can no longer write even a single line about her, except for the book's ending. My Urban Deconstruction lives exclusively in the long-term. It waits for the world's time to go by, whereas my novel unravels in a rather brief span of time, and at a certain point, it must find an end. The time of reality is nearly infinite, but that of narration is limited. Therefore, Zurlo's problem lies in this, Zandel who won't decide to die, and Marozia's in Clarissa, who barely talks to me anymore and doesn't answer my questions. She told me only that she has decided to go to Africa to treat people infected with AIDS with the Médecins Sans Frontières and that she wants to leave right away. Then she closed her eyes and said something horrible.

"And now I beg you to forget about me."

Africa will be the right atonement for her mental and sexual disorders and especially for a vulgar betrayal, unworthy of her and an infinite sorrow for me.

It's a soft and bright September, like Roman Septembers always are. The leaves of the lindens and sycamores are turning yellow. They stay hanging up there, and they will soon fall down at each light gust of wind. The air seems clean. I breathe, and this is a good thing because it means that I am alive and that I still have some desires. I would really like to go to the Casina Valadier and sit down to have tea with a person who loves me. I need love, but Clarissa can't give it to me. She's sick, sad and enraged, on her way to Africa. Nor can Valeria give it to me, since for some time she has been destined to offer me only light sexual shivers in a condo.

Zandel, if only I could talk to Zandel, but his illness has saddened and segregated him to the point that he doesn't want to see anybody for any reason. I know that Zandel's problem will just dissolve as can easily be foreseen, and it will make a conclusion for my novel, a very sad conclusion, but it's life that imprints my writing with this funereal seal, it's not me.

Certainly Clarissa's depression — this time it's not melancholy, this is a real, black depression or, better yet, a real, concave despair

— led to her decision to go to Africa and treat people infected with AIDS. It's the most intelligent thing she could have done in her situation. From the moment she had a sexual affair with that vulgar individual, only she is responsible for her destiny, and I can't help her. And if I could, would I help her? I don't know, and I don't want to think about it.

I wrote pages of literary fiction, but this is not fiction, unfortunately. It's reality, which once again has overcome and obliterated imagination, and now it imposes its conditions, its rhythms, its deadlines, like a pirate wind that sweeps away everything along with it. After Zandel's death I will wait for the death of the woman whom I love even though she betrayed me in such a vulgar way. I've understood that one can also love with pain, but this doesn't change a thing, because by now we are all defeated.

Honestly, I'd like it if my novel were never to find an ending, and instead, shortly, it will have found two, one in Rome and one in Mozambique.

This book has another possible ending. It can happen that an author might have some regret if the story leads one of his characters to come to a bad end. It also happens in life that someone dear is crushed by a bad destiny, but in a novel the author finds himself in the happy position of being empowered, with the aid of few words, to come to the rescue of a character, or rather of a person like Clarissa, who after many pages is by now dear to him, despite her whims and her awful behavior. In this "revised" version a temporary African punishment is imposed upon her, but I have saved her life.

"First ethics and then science." Is this perhaps the path I must follow ever since the moment I decided to write a novel? Ethics suggests that I respect Zandel's illness, whereas my narrative is telling me his life is only an obstacle and that, for this reason, there's nothing respectable about it.

Now Clarissa, too, has entered death row, and she no longer acts out her usual marital comedy but rather feels fully overwhelmed by tragedy. At this point I no longer want to write even a single line about her, except for the book's ending. She doesn't deserve so much attention. More than anything, I don't want to reveal to her that L.N.'s illness is my invention.

My Urban Deconstruction lives exclusively in the long-term. It waits for the world's time to go by, whereas my novel unravels in a rather brief span of time, and at a certain point, it must find an end. The time of reality is nearly infinite, but that of narration is limited. Therefore, Zurlo's problem lies in this, Zandel who won't decide to die, and Marozia's in Clarissa, who barely talks to me anymore and doesn't answer my questions. She told me only that she has decided to go to Africa to treat people infected with AIDS with the Médecins Sans Frontières and that she wants to leave right away. Then she closed her eyes and said something horrible.

"And now I beg you to forget about me."

Africa will be the right punishment for her mental and sexual disorders, her atonement for a vulgar betrayal, unworthy of her and an infinite sorrow for me. And when she realizes she's not sick, it will be up to her to decide what to do with her life.

It's a soft and bright September, like Roman Septembers always are. The leaves of the lindens and sycamores are turning yellow. They stay hanging up there, and they will soon fall down at each light gust of wind. The air seems clean. I breathe, and this is a good thing because it means that I am alive and that I still have some desires. I would really like to go to the Casina Valadier and sit down to have tea with a person who loves me. I need love, but Clarissa can't give it to me. She's sick, sad and enraged, and I am no longer able to touch her since she confirmed to me what I already knew, when she called that ugly individual Luccio, after they returned from their erotic trip to Barcelona. Our relationship ended because, whereas I reluctantly accepted her intimacy with Zandel, her sexual relationship with L.N. created a barrier between us that I will never be able to overcome. Since I first became suspicious, I no longer made love to Clarissa because my body refuses to enter where that horrible individual has entered. For now, I make do with Valeria, who for some time has been destined to offer me only light sexual shivers in a condo. But I still have a bit of future at my disposal.

Zandel, if only I could talk to Zandel, but his illness has saddened and segregated him to the point that he doesn't want to see anybody for any reason. I know that Zandel's problem will just dissolve as can easily be foreseen, and it will make a conclusion for my novel, a very sad conclusion, but it's life that imprints my writing with this funereal seal, it's not me.

Certainly Clarissa's depression — this time it's not melancholy, this is a real, black depression or, better yet, a real, concave despair — comes from the news she read in my book about Lucci Nerissi being HIV positive. If she's so worried, this is further confirmation, not necessary after all, that she had a sexual affair with him. So only she is responsible for her destiny, and I can't help her. And if I could, would I help her? Should I tell her the truth, that it's just an invention of mine? Actually no, she has to live out this dramatic experience until she realizes on her own that she isn't sick.

Clarissa no longer talks to me because she thinks I'm responsible for her misfortune. Should I have notified her about a nonexistent infection? She didn't even want to verify whether the news is true. After all, how could she? Whom could she have asked whether Lucci Nerissi is HIV positive? The news is credible in and of itself, just like all the facts recounted in my book are true and credible.

Clarissa made a decision that I believed to be wise in case she had contracted the infection, but I deem it wise even with no infection. As she told me, she will go to Africa, I believe to Mozambique, to treat people infected with AIDS with the Médecins Sans Frontières. Along with this information, she communicated her intention to withdraw a reasonable amount from the stock and bond package deposited in our bank. I approved of her plan, and let's hope that in Africa she won't contract the illness she thought she had contracted in Rome. But what do I care at this point? For me, Clarissa belongs to the past, and for her, I am a murderer.

I wrote pages of literary fiction, but this time fiction invaded reality, and now it imposes its conditions, its rhythms, its deadlines, like a pirate wind that sweeps away everything along with it. After

Zandel's death, I will still dedicate many thoughts to the woman whom I love even though she betrayed me in such a vulgar way and even though she begged me to forget about her. I have understood that one can also love with pain, but this doesn't change a thing, because by now we are all defeated.

Honestly, I'd like it if my novel were never to find an end, and instead, shortly, it will have found two, one in Rome and one in Mozambique.

NOTES

1. The name Gaio is also an Italian adjective, 'gaio', which means gay, as in happy.

2. "Il passero solitario" ("The Solitary Bird") is one of the best known poems by the prominent Italian poet, Giacomo Leopardi (1798–1837). "Passera" (*sparrow*) is a common colloquial metaphor for the female sexual organ.

3. Digos, the "Divisione investigazioni generali e operazioni speciali," is a special branch of the police department dealing with political security.

4. Malerba here reproduces a poem by Torquato Tasso (1544–95), a celebrated Italian poet of the late Renaissance. Written in madrigal form, "Qual rugiada o qual pianto" is one of his best known love poems, and Malerba quotes it in its entirety. We have followed the translation by Maria Pastore Passaro in *Rhymes of Love* (Ottawa: Legas, 2011), p. 179.

This Book Was Completed on 1 June 2017
At Italica Press, New York, New York.
It Was Set in Garamond and
Garamond Expert.

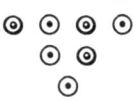

www.ingramcontent.com/pod-product-compliance
Lightning Source LLC
Chambersburg PA
CBHW030328020726
47493CB00004B/1200